CW01376132

ENDORSEMENTS

"Rodolfo Eyl (Rudi) is an incredible leader whose servant leadership and care for others shines through in everything that he does. It has and always will be a great honor to be Rudi's friend and colleague."

—Chris Martin, CEO at President at American Health Associates

"Very few stories have both the power to fully engage you and push you forward. *Holcan Code* is one such story–certain to transform lives."

—Carlos Pan, Chief Executive Officer at Accusys Technology

"This gastronomic novelty is packed with bitter truth, sweet revelation, and the spice of life: compassionate creation."

—José Vergara, President & Chief Operating Officer at Berkowitz Pollack Brant Advisors + CPAs

"Part memoir, part roadmap to self-development, this combo makes the *Holcan Code* a fantastic read! This heartwarming novel is highly recommended for young adults looking to find a purpose in life."

—José León Padilla, Associate at Goldman Sachs

"*Holcan Code* does something meaningful: it champions a cause that matters, at first, to challenge our mindset far and wide; *Holcan Code* then achieves something hard: it smooths out those thoughts with foolproof logic and points out a direction to a newfound plan. A powerful journey that establishes the impact of determination and will towards betterment of future generations."

—JOHN FEDELE, CEO AT GOLDEN SANDS GENERAL CONTRACTORS, INC.

"When you feel that you've created an emotional connection with the characters, the book you read was no doubt extraordinary. This book will not leave any reader the same–Find out for yourself!"

—ERIC TODD LEVIN, CHAIRMAN AT ATLANTIC TRACTOR

"Yab's real-life rags-to-riches tale is sure to leave you hungry for change."

—MARK ZACAPA, CEO AT EXIID INTERNATIONAL

"It's one thing to call for major change and another completely–like Rudi–to truly lead the march."

—FERNANDO CASTILLO, CEO / CO-FOUNDER AT RAÍZ CAPITAL

"Like spice sensation Yab's own dishes, *Holcan Code* is flavorful and wholesome, crafted with love."

—Edi Fellmann, Founder & CEO at Asociación Nuevo Amanecer

"I like how the author sees the world—applying truth and morality as his guiding principle—and the way in which he makes the main character interact with the world around him—the way he thinks and feels. This story truly leaves us with a great legacy."

—René Guillén, Food Serial Entrepreneur in Madrid, Spain

"Rudi's always been a natural storyteller and a powerful communicator; and when you add a beautifully illustrated booklet to this mix, you get *Holcan Code*—a delightful reading experience."

—Dev Chanchani, Partner at XIP, LLC

"Hard work, grit and determination are a few of the things that come to mind when thinking about Rudi's attitude when undertaking any project—and even as a first-time author—*Holcan Code* is not an exception. This book has the power to awaken the entrepreneur that every reader carries inside."

—Jose Pineda Flores, Chief Legal Officer at FINCA

HOLCAN CODE

A Migrant's Journey to Creating
Abundance for Many

RODOLFO EYL CUEVA

HOLCAN CODE
A Migrant's Journey to Creating Abundance for Many

Copyright © 2022 Rodolfo Eyl Cueva. All rights reserved.

ISBN 978-1-66785-128-0 (Print)
ISBN 978-1-66785-129-7 (eBook)

No part of this publication may be reproduced, distributed, or transmitted in any form or by any means, including photocopying, recording, or other electronic or mechanical methods, without the prior written permission of the author, except in the case of brief quotations embodied in critical reviews and certain other noncommercial uses permitted by copyright law.

TABLE OF CONTENTS

SUMMARY i
FOREWORD iii
PREFACE v
ACKNOWLEDGEMENTS xiii
DEDICATION xv
Chapter 1: STRONG ROOTS 1
Chapter 2: THE ORIGIN OF ABUNDANCE 13
Chapter 3: THE MAYAN SPINNER (PART ONE) 27
Chapter 4: THE MAYAN SPINNER (PART TWO) 45
Chapter 5: THE CARAVAN TO THE US 57
Chapter 6: VICTOR'S DINER 67
Chapter 7: THE SHELTER 75
Chapter 8: TASTES LIKE THE REAL DEAL 83
Chapter 9: THE WARRIOR AWAKENS 91
Chapter 10: RE-GOALED & RE-ENERGIZED 97
Chapter 11: YAB'S MOUNT OLYMPUS 109
Chapter 12: ANOTHER TEST 113
Chapter 13: INTERNAL DIALOGUE STORM 121
Chapter 14: IMPACT INVESTMENT VENTURE CHALLENGE ... 135
Chapter 15: THE OFFICIAL START-UP MAGAZINE 147
Chapter 16: THE SPICE SOCIETY 155
Chapter 17: WHITE SMOKE 177
Chapter 18: A TASTE OF HOME WHEREVER YOU ARE 197
Chapter 19: A PLATFORM THAT ELIMINATES
SYSTEMIC POVERTY 215
Chapter 20: THE CEIBA TREE 221

SUMMARY

With a Mayan artifact in his pocket, a mantra in his mind, and a passionate goal in his heart, a young, ambitious man leaves Copan in search of a brighter future in the US, not only for himself but all the people waiting back home.

A servant leader, a life-long learner, and a man who doesn't back down from any challenge, Yab is equipped for success, standing upon the shoulders of his family and forebears. The dream, however, is daunting, indeed, as building a bridge between the US and his homeland won't be easy.

Planting the seeds of prosperity for one and all will require one thing: deciphering the Holcan Code–a relic of the past that holds the key to a brighter future

FOREWORD

Life is full of seeming paradoxes. *To move forward, we must look back. Personal happiness is contingent upon serving others. Compassion demands competition.* The list goes on, but a trend is apparent: the power of connectivity. We don't win alone but by honoring where we came from, bringing others up as we seek solutions to benefit all. This timeless code contains the knowledge needed to alter Earth completely–and, at heart, it's truly simple to crack.

Together, we'll do just that.

The tale that follows is certainly meant to entertain. It has every component required to do so: a fearless underdog, a wild vision, a perilous journey, and endless obstacles. There is, however, a greater instructive purpose involved: imagination–not in the sense of escapism, no, but rather conceiving of latent real-world splendor and striving to bring it about. This piece of artwork imitates life, and readers are, too, invited to drink of its knowledge, pushing forward, inspired, to further Yab's pure goal.

The time has come to part ways with the old paradigm and start making connections on a human level. It won't be easy by any means, but knowing where we're headed *is*.

We need only aim for a future in which no soul feels forced to flee their homeland. A future in which connection first and foremost defines our common spirit–and not by top-down globalist force but human-to-human interaction, preserving eclectic cultures en route.

So, if you're accustomed to passive observance, dear reader, be ready for something different. This isn't but a narrative. It's a challenge and a "call to charms." You may not have a Mayan spinner, but guided by sound principles, there's nothing that you can't dream or do. Remember, when you reach the end, your journey is only beginning …

–María Elena Bottazzi, Co-Director at Texas Children's Hospital Center for Vaccine Development at Baylor College of Medicine

PREFACE

Fragment of "La Patria" by Ventura Ruiz Aguilera

One day I wanted to learn
what the Homeland is,
I was told by an old man
Who loved it dearly:

One feels the homeland;
There are no words
In human tongues
that can clearly explain it.

»There, where all
Things speak to us
With a resounding voice
That penetrates our soul;

»There, where the
first day starts
That to men in the world
The heavens point out to;

»Memories, loves,
Sadness, hopes,
That have been sources
of joys and sorrows

Ask if it can
Ever be forgotten,
If in vigil and sleep
For it they cry not!

There is not, to the eyes,
A more beautiful place
Neither in field nor sky
None equals it.

Fragmento de "La Patria" por Ventura Ruiz Aguilera

Queriendo yo un dia
Saber qué es la Pátria,
Me dijo un anciano
Que mucho la amaba:

«La Patria se siente;
No tienen palabras
Que claro la expliquen
Las lenguas humanas.

»Allí, donde todas
Las cosas nos hablan
Con voz que hasta el fondo
Penetra del alma;

»Allí, donde empieza
La breve jornada
Que al hombre en el mundo
Los cielos señalan;

»Recuerdos, amores,
Tristeza, esperanzas,
Que fuentes han sido
De gozos y lágrimas;

»Pregunta si pueden
Jamás olvidarla,
Si en sueño y vigilia
Por ella no claman!

»No existe, á sus ojos,
Más bella morada,
Ni en campo ni en cielo
Ninguna le iguala.

    Do you care deeply about the future of your country and/or community? Do you dedicate the results of your work and your hard-won achievements–no matter how small–to your people? Do you feel it's your responsibility to make your community and/or country better–even if you have migrated and currently live abroad? Do you wish to pass on the love you feel for your homeland to your children? If you answered yes to these questions, you have the heart to become a Holcan warrior, and this book will share with you what principles are required to become one.

A Holcan warrior defends his people and his homeland with all his might–regardless of his current country of residence. He is a citizen of the world that explores new territories with the intention of improving lives back home. A Holcan warrior is a go-getter–what we call in Spanish, a *luchador*–and always has clear goals. Holcan warriors were the most effective fighting forces of the Mayan Civilization. They would secure trading routes for the benefit of their entire civilization. They had one job–which they invested themselves entirely in. To protect their land and its community.

While these were fearless and admirable characters who were respected by society, becoming a Holcan warrior came at a high price. A Holcan warrior has to have a thematic and clear goal, which has to be inclusive of the interests of the warrior's neighbors, seeking to help society at large.

True Holcan warriors protect what's most valued by their peers from the gravest dangers. Nowadays, in the face of such recurring issues, and out of desperation, fellow Latin Americans choose to leave their countries at all costs–which leads to illegal immigration–a phenomenon that leaves everybody on the losing side: suffering immigrants that feel forced to leave their homes, broken families left behind, and the host countries, which are left to deal with the lives of real people with all sorts of different motivations and interests–a wearisome endeavor, to say the least.

In view of this, for all those readers with Holcan hearts, it is our job as an International Holcan Tribe to battle this common issue…by making the world a better place and providing opportunity.

A non-negotiable characteristic of a warrior is resourcefulness, or as a Holcan Warrior would call it, "a creative mind." This concept essentially represents our ability to overcome anything through creative thinking and effective problem-solving.

Throughout the battles you've fought as a warrior, you've probably already experienced a taste of the wonders that this vital ability can bring to life. A creative mind can overcome any enemy troop or obstacle.

This manuscript is my invitation for you and other Holcan warriors across the globe to join the fight against the issues that cause illegal immigration. We've identified a common enemy, and through the use of *my* creative mind, I've managed to come up with a long-term, replicable solution that I'd like to share with you, as it may prove just the inspiration you need in your respective industry or business sector. It's a platform-based business solution that interconnects all of the stakeholders affected by illegal immigration and allows them to work as a team. My platform is called Spice Society, and it's what this book is about.

Entrepreneurs and moral consumers, the problem that we face today will never be solved by walls but by *bridges*. Together, connected, we're sure to succeed–so join our movement today!

The Collapse of Copan in western Honduras is believed to have occurred sometime between 800 and 830 AD. Some archeologists have concluded that the lack of sustainability practices in the valley and the fact that the Mayans consumed all of their natural resources is what forced the population to migrate to nearby Yucatan. My mother is from the beautiful Copan Ruins. I love Copan dearly. The area is splendorous; the soil is fertile and the land full of opportunities; yet most of its local young men have immigrated to the US and Spain. Back in Mayan times, Mexico was able to absorb the fleeing Copan Population, but I don't think the US and Spain will be able to do so in present times. The burden created on its healthcare, education, and security among other factors is huge. I feel the responsibility to avoid another collapse of Copan.

Almost ten years ago, at HBS OPM 43, Prof. Lynda Applegate kindly challenged me to better structure my social responsibility efforts in my home country. She warned me about not just becoming a traditional non-profit donor/volunteer and inspired me to begin my own sustainable community in Honduras. Upon graduation, I went on to vertically integrate my food business with small pepper and spice growers in the remote mountains on the Honduras/Guatemala border. Our Agro platform has now grown to five hundred land-owner families with the short-term plan of including a total of 2000 families and exporting plant-based foods to various parts of the world.

WHO WAS THIS BOOK WRITTEN FOR?

- Those worried about the effects illegal immigration is having in your community and would like to do something about it through business.

- Parties interested in impact investing.

- LATAM entrepreneurs–and the generations to come–who export products around the world, generating thousands of jobs in their homelands.

- The countless migrants who leave their homelands in pursuit of achieving such sizable success that will allow them to share with those back home.

- Businessmen who transfer know-how, technology, and, in sum, progress to their communities.

- Successful professionals who have achieved greatness in their respective fields by putting their education and values from back home into practice abroad.

- To the students who dream about studying abroad and bringing back knowledge and creating a better world.

ACKNOWLEDGEMENTS

I would like to thank many who have made this book possible.

To my wife, Regina: You have inspired my life with love since we were fourteen years old.

To my mother, Elia Sara Cueva: Thank you for instilling your social-worker heart in me. I admire your work for others.

To my father, Antonio Rodolfo Eyl: Thank you for being my role model and for being an example of hard work, solid moral values and always being kind to others.

To my kids, Antonella, Rudi, and Roderick: Never forget where we come from and to do good for our people.

To Prof. Lynda Applegate: Thank you for creating a replacement picture of how I can serve my community and make it sustainable.

To our business leadership and all of our team members: None of this would be possible without your hard work and passion for our group.

To Tia Flavia Elisa: Thank you for helping me re-create the cherished moments I had with your father and for sharing our love for Copan with a whole new generation.

To our agro-partners: This is just the beginning; thank you for trusting us.

To our customers: You make the platform work, and it all starts with you.

To Jose Armando Berlioz Melgar: Working with you on the book has been remarkable; I admire your intelligence, values, and hard work. Thank you, and thanks to our angel inspiring us from heaven.

To Andrea Cabrera and Fernado Lopez: Thank you for the book's beautiful illustrations; I know many will enjoy them.

To my YPO Forum: Thank you for your support all these years.

DEDICATION

In memory of my uncle,
Dr. Adan Cueva Villamil.

*Thank you for being my grandfather.
I cherish the love, kindness and
enthusiasm you had for others.
I miss your wonderful stories
about the Mayans!*

1

STRONG ROOTS

With his hands full with two overstuffed grocery bags, Yab strolled down the tree-lined, cobbled street, whistling a cheerful tune. *It's a beautiful day,* Yab thought, staring at the golden-pink, slowly dusking sky where a lone cloud was drifting away.

Sweat gleamed on his forehead and his hands shook with exhaustion, but Yab's smile was beaming. It was that special moment of the month again when Yab would visit the local chicken farmers and the spice and pepper producers to hand-pick the food for his restaurant. His love for his clientele was such that he wouldn't let anyone else choose the food that was going into his customers' plates. He wanted only the best for them. The neighborhood's butcher and the grocery store owner surely knew their crafts, but as thoughtful as he was, he had to make sure that every single element was chosen with care. No one could tell the difference between the regular chicken and the pasture-raised like he did. So, he only trusted the local producers and his very own eyes. He picked only the freshest chicken—ones with a specific diet—and the most fragrant chili peppers, along with just the best of the lot: bean proteins, plantains, natural gums, pumpkin seeds, and yuca. Half of his cooking relied on the excellence of the natural ingredients, and his customers loved his recipes for that reason.

Skipping with enthusiasm, Yab turned down the main street hastily, eager to experiment with the new chili powder he wanted to use as a condiment for his breaded chicken recipe. The sign he recently installed appeared in the distance, flashing green and orange, drawing the customers in.

As he approached the restaurant's entrance, the door burst open violently. Two men, dressed in black, lurched outside, faces veiled behind ski masks. Yab froze at the sight of holstered guns in their belts, the grocery bags falling off his arms. It wasn't the first time he'd had to witness that sight. As a matter of fact, it was the third time in the restaurant's brief history. Yab knew better than to confront them. Last time, the robbers whole-heartedly offered him a scar and more than a few bruises.

Yab stood still, watching the robbers clench their heavy backpacks and jump on their parked bikes.

"Go, go, go!" the robber shouted to the driver.

The engine revved, and the bike sped off into the distance, taking a sharp turn, fleeing the chaos that had been left behind. People stood aghast, murmuring, pointing toward the restaurant. Despite the initial shock, it was a normal day for most people there. Yab had heard of over a hundred such incidents taking place in the neighborhood over the past few months alone.

When the initial shock faded, Yab bolted into the restaurant.

The customers were pale, their faces still on the ground and their hands behind their heads, some crying and sobbing, others lying in whimpering silence, not daring to lift their gaze from the floor. No one moved as if they were a collection of mortified statues.

Yab's right-hand man, shaking like the last winter leaf, risked a peek behind the counter.

"Manuel!" Yab called out.

"Boss," Manuel said with tears in his eyes, stepping around the counter apprehensively. "They took their money, their phones, and everything we had in the register. I-I...I couldn't stop them!"

Yab noticed a swollen, red patch on Manuel's head.

"Everyone!" Yab announced, turning to the customers, deeply concerned. "I'm terribly sorry for your trouble. This is a shameful situation–the one you just went through–but since no one's hurt, please go home to your families; your meals today are on me."

Yab turned to Manuel.

"They took everything," Manuel said again. "All the money."

"Screw the money," Yab helped Manuel to his feet and looked at his bruised head. "Let me get a bandage for that."

"I tried to stop them," Manuel murmured again, obviously in shock.

"I'm just glad everyone's okay," Yab said, cleaning the wound and wrapping a bandage around it.

Most of the customers left once they made sure that it was safe to return to the street, leaving Yab's restaurant a mess: plates still half-full chairs and tables strewn on the ground among fragments of broken glass.

"Let me help you clean up," Manuel said.

"Go home, Manuel," Yab ordered. "We'll do that tomorrow, okay?"

"Are you sure?"

Yab nodded. "Yes, go get some rest, please."

Manuel thanked Yab and left him alone in the ransacked restaurant. Yab dropped into a chair and sighed deeply, staring at the empty cash register. Last time, the register had been almost empty when the robbers appeared. Today, they'd managed to take the entire day's earnings and ruined everyone's meal.

Money was the last of Yab's concerns. His company was thriving, and he could use some of his savings to repay the damages. Yab was upset they had hurt Manuel and yet again ruined everyone's day at his restaurant. Yab was disgusted at the new reality that had been forming in the area the past few years. He rubbed his eyes and dropped into a chair, exhaling sharply. What was he supposed to do? Most of his entrepreneur friends made sure to hire private security–but that ran way past his budget–and some even paid the gang members to avoid trouble. They paid the same people that ruined lives to secure theirs.

Only Yab saw that as madness? He always insisted that as long as people condoned this criminal mentality, things would keep getting worse. Ostensibly, he was the only one paying the real price, due to his ideals.

With his mood ruined, Yab closed and barred the restaurant while the sunset behind the mountains threw off fiery light, blanketing the Latin American forests, adding a golden hue to the leaves and branches. Despite the drab colors of his afternoon, Yab managed to keep a positive attitude and knew that God was in control, helping him get through the ups and downs of his life.

The sight of the scenery's uncanny beauty snatched a smile out of him–which got him thinking: At least he didn't have to work late that day, hidden in his kitchen, and instead he could appreciate nature's beauty.

Yab entered his home and nodded at his father.

"You're home early," his father remarked.

"Two robbers struck the restaurant today," Yab said indifferently, almost numb from the situation.

"Did they hurt you?" asked his father and attempted to get off his chair.

"No, no, I wasn't there when it happened. They hit Manuel though. They better not set their foot in the restaurant again. Coming after the restaurant is one thing, but coming after my people is another. I can't stand for that."

His father started mumbling about the criminal activity of the area, as thieves had recently affected his coffee plantation too, which all the more made him long for the old days when things were simple and more peaceful. Yab ignored his father's remarks and grabbed a bottle of orange juice from the fridge and downed three long gulps.

"Yab!" his father called out again from the living room. "I'm talking to you!"

"What is it, dad?"

"I said, you have a letter!"

Yab felt a rush running through him. Could it be the day he'd been longing for?

"Where is it?" Yab darted into the living room with anticipation.

"Hold your horses," his father said, from his comfortable armchair and pointed toward the table. "Over there."

Yab grabbed the letter and inspected the top right corner; which read "RNPM." The envelope trembled between his anxious fingertips, but he tore it open and pulled out the letter.

He skimmed through the unnecessary introductions and reached the bottom of the page, reading hungrily. Upon reaching the first few words of the closing remarks, however, Yab's smile faded, settling into a deep, perplexed frown.

"What's the matter?" his father asked, sensing his distress.

Knees buckling under the weight of what he'd just read, Yab fell back into the sofa and sighed deeply.

"You look like you've seen a ghost!" his father remarked, now worried, leaning forward.

Yab ignored his father for a moment, reading the letter again.

We are sorry to inform you that an identical formula has already been registered and is owned by the Government Food for the People Program. If you wish, you may present another submission with a substantially different formula for our office to evaluate.

Registro Nacional de Patentes y Marcas (RNPM).

How could the Government Food Program already own his invention? That was his creation! *His* idea. It wasn't possible. Yab and Dominic had been working on the plant-based chicken nuggets for months. They were about to secure the patent, and take their business to new lengths. There was something wrong.

Yab lurched off the sofa and grabbed the phone, typing with shivering fingers a number he knew by heart.

"Dominic?" Yab asked the moment the line stopped ringing. "Dominic, are you there?"

"I'm sorry, Yab," Dominic's sister said. "Dominic didn't come in today."

"Where is he?" Yab asked, his heart skipping a fearful beat.

The rustling of a dog barking filled the brief silence. "He didn't tell us where he was going. Do you want me to inform him about your call?"

"No, thank you," said Yab and hung up the phone, staring at his reflection on the dark screen. He *did* look like he'd seen a ghost.

"Will you tell me what's wrong?" his father insisted, alarmed by Yab's behavior.

"Dad, do you remember the plant-based chicken nuggets?" Yab asked.

His father smiled. "How wouldn't I? The vegan ones that taste like real chicken!"

"Well," Yab said. "It's lost. Someone already submitted the formula…*my* formula!"

His father shared an empathetic frown. He opened his mouth and closed it again but said nothing.

The room was suffocating Yab as if the letter had drained all the oxygen from the house. He needed to breathe. Yab dropped the letter and hurried out to the yard, where he began pacing in the small garden his father tended with so much care and passion.

Yab's feet were getting wet in the grass's fresh dew, but he couldn't sit. He couldn't relax. He took a deep breath, letting the flower-scented aroma quell his seething emotions.

How did this happen? There had to be a perfectly reasonable explanation. Dominic filed the motion to save him the trouble, right?

If that was the case, then why was it owned by the government's Food for the People Program? It just made no sense. There was something wrong. Why would they both file the patent?

It took them a few good years to perfect the plant-based nuggets, from conception to final product. Would all that go to waste?

Yab turned and saw the old wooden table in the middle of the garden, sitting under the thick nightshade of the blooming tree branches hanging over it like a canopy.

That's where they had come up with the idea. Yab remembered it as if it was unfolding now before him. They were young and ambitious back then, full of life and excitement. They used to spend hours together, talking and laughing till morning, and amongst those beautiful memories, the idea for the plant-based nuggets came to be, which he remembered perfectly:

"Dominic, both our fathers are coffee producers," Yab said. "Things worked out for them more or less, right? They joined the expanding market when it was still early!"

"Yeah, if by 'worked out' you mean the earn less every year. The intermediaries and the coffee roasters and retailers keep most of the profits," Dominic said sarcastically. "Our fathers make nothing out of it!"

"That's not the point," Yab corrected him. "Coffee is a $100 billion global industry, man. My dream is that we identify the next big business, perhaps as huge as the coffee industry, while catering to an unserved market! Imagine how proud our fathers would be!"

"My father always told me that I'd fail in life," Dominic snarked. "Well, he could have been right."

"My father always told me I'd succeed," Yab said. "I'll help you prove your father wrong and you'll help me prove my father right."

They shared a laugh before Yab continued.

"I truly believe we can set off an economic revolution and change our lives, man!"

"You always like to dream big, Yab, but it's easier said than done," Dominic replied with a contemplative gaze. "There aren't many things humanity hasn't discovered. It was easier back then, to make new discoveries. Now, not so much…"

"No, that's the pitfall, can't you see?" Yab argued. "If we accept that there is nothing new to invent, we're doomed. There are so many things we don't know–that we can't even fathom. That's the beauty of entrepreneurship, right? To see something no one else has! I bet all the famous inventors thought that way! All we have to do is look closely. We have been talking about how we want to be entrepreneurs and businessmen since we were boys, don't you remember?"

"I never truly believed that," Dominic said.

"We are in the perfect age and era to succeed," Yab said. "I still have that dream."

They argued about it, with Dominic contending that nothing new existed in the world and Yab adamantly disagreeing. It became a bet between them. Dominic challenged him to come up with something equally promising as coffee. "Well… what's popular nowadays? Where could we shove our noses in?" Yab pondered.

"Shove our noses where? The culinary world is out of new things," Dominic insisted. If you want to create something new these days, then you'll have to think of technology: virtual reality, artificial intelligence, robots, and stuff, you know? Yab thought about it for a moment with his mind coming up dry. It wasn't an easy task. Dominic kept looking at him with an arrogant smile.

"See?" Dominic said with a smirk. "There's nothing left to do…"

"I bet there is," Yab insisted, now thinking harder.

Yab turned and saw the vast fields unfolding from the edge of his house and extending as far as the eye could see. *Plants,* Yab thought, and the idea flashed in his mind like a firework.

"Plants!" Yab finally exclaimed. "You know how popular vegan and flexitarian diets have become these days; well, I already own a chicken restaurant, so I bet I could make a plant-based chicken as good as the real one!"

"How is this going to help?" Dominic asked.

"It's everywhere on social media, the news, everywhere," Yab said. "It's becoming a real trend! Imagine if you could have the option to eat a plant-based alternative that tasted equally as good as the original one. It's one of those things that sounds too good to be true, isn't it? For the people whose ideologies and diets won't allow them to eat real chickens, at least. They're getting the best of both worlds.

Think about it: Pasture-raised chicken feed from grass, so essentially they are nurtured through plants and; in a way, they're even made out of them. Here in Mayan lands, we've been blessed with the best soil, nutrients, and light, which means we could probably cook some seriously tasty plant-based chicken alternatives!

The idea stuck with them, and when making a list of all the benefits–including the fact that this would not only be nutritional for the consumers but also very affordable–Yab and Dominic realized that they had something important in their hands. Something *worthwhile*. It was a healthy, highly affordable solution, accessible to even the poorest souls, and it could be very appealing to children and parents who wanted to "trick" their children into eating more vegetables. It was an idea that had already exploded in the US and Europe, but the taste and texture of the vegan products weren't as good just yet. This was their chance to break into the market from a slightly different angle.

No wonder the Government Food Program wanted it, Yab thought, taking a seat at the bench. It was a great idea—one they had worked on with love and passion. But how had the government gotten its hands on it?

Yab picked up his phone and called Dominic again. Two rings later, Dominic picked up.

"Dominic," Yab said anxiously. "Did you receive a letter from RNPM?"

"No," Dominic said awkwardly. "I'm sorry, Yab."

Dominic's voice was somber, almost guilty. Yab remained silent, waiting for Dominic to explain.

"I'm sorry, but they paid me good money for it…" Dominic started to explain.

"You didn't…You stole the formula?" Yab murmured, panting with livid anger.

"The Government Food Board had me against the wall. They knew you wouldn't sell, so they approached me," Dominic murmured in a defeated whisper.

Cold silence followed.

"I'm sorry that it had to end this way, but it was either that or they threatened to find a way to get their hands on it, leaving me out with no money in exchange and I put too much time into this; Yab you're just too idealistic for your own good. I'm in this for the money; always have been," Dominic said.

Yab simply hung up, saying nothing. He was angry, frustrated, but what was the point of beating up Dominic? It would only make things worse. It was all over anyway.

This project had been like a child to him. He was in love with all of it: the numerous farmers that helped him grow the perfect food to make the formula right, the late nights perfecting the recipe, and all of the blind taste tests. It was the project and the process he had fallen in love with, even if he got nothing in return. And just like that, the project was gone.

His father joined him out in the yard with two cups of coffee, taking a seat at the table, pushing one across the table.

"Sit," his father said simply, taking a sip of the hot brew.

"I'm not in the mood for coffee," Yab said.

"*Sit*," his father insisted in a stern but compassionate tone.

Yab sat across from him, took the cup in his hands, and let the fragrance alleviate his pain.

"So?" his father asked patiently. "What happened?"

Yab hesitated. He was in no mood to discuss what had happened, but his father would keep insisting.

"Three times," Yab said. "Three times, and that's how all my efforts end up. A total failure!"

"Failure is a very strong word, son," his father said.

"You think? My ideas have been exploited by Dominic *and* the government. It can't get any closer to failure than that…"

His father took a slow sip, listening peacefully.

"You told me my name means abundance in Mayan, no?" Yab said. "Well, I don't see any abundance here."

2

THE ORIGIN OF ABUNDANCE

"Son, let's calm down and talk this out," Yab's father said in a deep, strong voice. "Let me provide some background: Did you know that ever since your mom was born, she has been participating in your family's ritual of the maize god, Hun Hunahpu? "At the beginning of each planting season, the sculpture is placed under the huge ceiba tree at your Abuelo's farm. Do you know which tree this is? "

Yab rolled his eyes in annoyance. Yet another story from the Mayan times was about to begin. Yab was tired of those.

"The significance of the ritual for the family was seeking an abundance of wellness and well-being through the new harvest. Think about it, Yab: every harvest creates new life!"

Yab responded angrily, "For crying out loud, Dad! I don't have time for this; Manuel is probably still traumatized in his house because of me. I'm sick and tired of this land, and you continue to promote it. Just for once, admit it's not as good as you claim it is. Times have changed; there's no need to maintain this false optimism."

"You certainly have an attitude on you, young man, but I'll let it slide because I know how tough the day has been for you. Come on, hear your old man out. All these stories I tell you are true, and they're also funny. They'll cheer you up!"

"They're never funny, Dad..." Yab sighed.

"I bet I can make you laugh a little bit. Come on–give me a chance."

"Fine..." said Yab, who really wasn't in the mood for stories but still didn't want to go against his father's wishes. He got so much joy from telling those stories, and Yab could certainly use a distraction if nothing else.

"Let's go back to the maize god: Every new season begins with a *healthy seed,* and your Abuelo would place a whole sack of these seeds at the base of the ceiba tree next to the sculpture. The kernels would then be planted the following day."

"Why under the ceiba trees?" Yab asked.

"To the Mayans, ceiba trees were sacred," his father responded. "It was believed that its huge tree roots reached the underworld. Supposedly, by putting the sack of seeds in contact with the ceiba tree's soil, the soon-to-be planted crop would receive special favor from the gods that would bless its growth and make it as solid and stern as the ceiba tree."

"I'm not getting the point, Dad", Yab said.

Yab's father got to thinking about how he could convey his message more effectively to his son. This was a valuable lesson that he yearned for him to understand. "Let me draw it out for you, Son! In essence, the tree is simply a metaphor that our family has used throughout generations to teach us about work values."

Yab's father went on to draw a small seed that transformed into a huge trunk. He sketched the robust branches, the canopy, and some acorns. Afterward, he recapped. "The initial ritual I explained to you is so complex because beginnings, Yab, are key for a journey's success. How and where they're planted will determine the quality of its fruit.

"And, just like seeds, work will only produce good results if planted in fertile soil and with the right timing. The seed is the foundation of everything and–when planted adequately–it will produce strong roots, which will become big and stable, and help sustain the mighty tree that is yet to come and all that it represents.

"Therefore, the seeds and its roots represent *honest-disciplined work*. Let me explain: Similar to a ceiba tree's immense roots–seemingly unbreakable–honest work creates pillars that are so strong that they're also indestructible. Think about it, Son. No one can dispute the work of honest hands and sweaty foreheads; and that, my boy, is how your family has built its legacy."

Yab pictured a ceiba tree in all its grandeur. But he just rolled his eyes impatiently.

"Now, having expanded its beautiful roots, the tree slowly starts to develop its solid trunk, which represents *expertise in a specific area*. You've heard this thousands of times: Mayans sought to be masters of their crafts, whatever it was that they pursued as a goal. This leaves us an important principle to live by: We need to seek to become experts of whatever it is that we are passionate about and choose to dedicate our lives to.

"Take my father, for example–he's one of the best coffee-growers in these lands; but that only came as a result of his hard work, learning all that he could. He was up before sunrise and didn't leave the fields until sunset. And this, my son, is what allowed him to become such an expert in this area.

"Thirdly, the branches that sprout from the trunk represent the multiple processes that a business venture undergoes in order to become the *best in their class* and eventually achieve *world-class quality* in whatever it is that they do."

Yab looked puzzled. *The branches represent the processes,* he thought with a distant look in his eyes.

His father caught his confusion and tried to explain. "Yab, answer this question for me please: what type of tree has more branches, a big one or a small one?" Yab had had enough of his dad's riddles, but very hesitantly, he took a deep breath and replied, "The big one, Dad. The big one…"

"Bear with me, Son. So, it's safe to say that the bigger a tree gets, the more branches it grows, right?"

"Well, only if taken good care of," Yab said.

"That's it, Yab! You hit the nail on the head! As healthy businesses grow, their processes also multiply, just like branches on a growing tree, in order to adapt to the growing demand and to adjust to the constantly higher quality standards expected by the markets!"

Yab nodded. "Okay, I see where you're going…It's actually not such a bad metaphor, Dad."

"Not bad? It's tremendous, Yab! You see, when a company starts experiencing success to any degree, that's actually just the very beginning. The real challenge is making such success sustainable. So, here's where the branches come along. After we learn that something works, we work hard to see how to make it even better in every aspect. We ask ourselves questions such as: how can we make our target client love our product even more? How can we get involved with more social causes through our projects? How can we offer our farmers even better conditions? How can we offer our team a better lifestyle? And ultimately, how do we become the best professionals in the world? And then we repeat this process over and over again until we achieve excellence across the ever-changing standards established by culture, technological advances, generational trends, and the latest information.

"Fourth come the acorns, and now listen closely because this is where your name is introduced to the story, my son, for Yab means *abundance.*

"In the initial ceremony I was telling you about earlier, your abuela would shout out loud, in the Mayan language. 'Give us Yab this season! Bless us with Yab!' She was whole-heartedly pleading for abundance for the family and the entire town, and the truth is, believe it or not, it always worked. Although many thought she was crazy," Dad said, chuckling playfully, "she was a woman of strong faith.

"But your abuela felt so overabundantly blessed, she couldn't help but share these traditions with everyone she could; she firmly believed that the abundance of the land was enough to provide for everyone, so she gifted seeds and even ceiba tree acorns to everyone! So, she would insist that the other families of the community replicate the entire ceiba tree ceremony…and what do you think happened? As neighbors started believing in it and putting it into practice, their households started to flourish, little by little."

Yab's dad caught him staring at the open space, distracted. "Planet Earth calling Yab," his father said jokingly, as he saw that Yab had been distracted by his own thoughts.

"Sorry! I just never knew that part. I guess it's about time for me to *branch* out!"

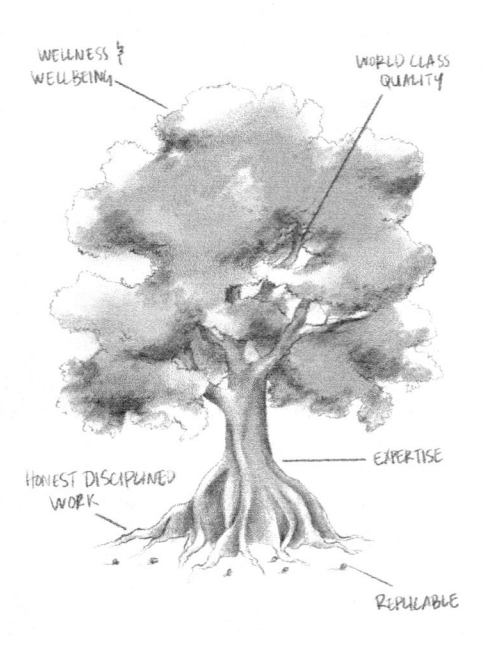

Tree diagram with labels: WELLNESS & WELL-BEING, WORLD CLASS QUALITY, HONEST DISCIPLINED WORK, EXPERTISE, REPLICABLE

Lame joke notwithstanding, Yab's father was pleased to see the boy's mood improving, and he laughed heartily before continuing. "So, finally…guess what the fifth and final work value is in the ceiba tree? It's the tree's canopy. Its beautiful cone-shaped leaves represent the family's *wellness and well-being*," he said, pointing at the tree's canopy. "You see how it all serves a perfect and specific purpose in the tree's growth cycle and makes it work so well together? Take a look at the canopy; even its shape is suggestive of protection and comfort like a bed. All that we do and strive for, Yab, would be insignificant if we and our community weren't blessed enough to have wellness and well-being."

Yab scoffed. "I have to admit, this story *is* uplifting, Dad, and these values can be applied to any project–not just planting."

"It might be hard for you to see it right now, but despite the robbery today and despite everything bad that has happened, you are, in fact, a very blessed young man."

"How am I blessed, Dad?"

"You may not be ready to understand the meaning of all these Mayan stories, but as you grow, with time and experience, you'll discover how they apply to you, and I trust that being the intelligent young man you are, you'll be able to replicate the methods that lead you to success many times and create abundance for many.

"Let me show you something."

Yab's father stormed back to the house and put up a wooden ladder to reach the top drawers of the closet in his room. "Aha!" he said as if having deciphered a secret. Yab overheard his excitement all the way from the porch.

What crazy business is he going to come up with this time? Yab thought, unbothered.

Racing back from inside the house came Yab's father with an old paper folder. He carefully blew off the dust and opened it, showing Yab a pencil drawing. "Bear with me for a while longer, okay?"

"Fine..."

"You know, Yab, this is serious stuff. The Mayans went through terrible droughts, famines, and other terrible situations–things that were way worse than what you're going through right now. "This is the maize god and it was one of the most important gods to the Mayans. Even nowadays, he continues to be a pillar to Mayan descendants, since corn is Copán's major crop."

Yab's Father began giggling. "I was told that from the very first time your mother saw Hun Hunapnu's, when she was five years old, she fell in love with him, as he appeared youthful, vibrant, and handsome. From all the shouting and praising of your abuela, your mom nicknamed the statue *Yab*."

"Your mother, imitating your abuela, shouted 'Yab! Yab!' while she danced around it, and she made so much noise, the whole neighborhood could hear her!" Yab's father said, now laughing.

A shy smile crept on the edge of Yab's lips.

"And that, my son, is where your name comes from. Although, you are much more handsome than Hun Hunahpu–no doubt of that," his father said and chuckled.

Yab chuckled as well.

"See, I told you you would laugh!" his father remarked with pride. "I bet you never would have guessed that you are somehow connected to a romance between corn, rebirth, and abundance, Son; you see, every day is good for starting a new cycle–for renovation."

Yab wasn't really feeling comforted, but he wouldn't strip the pride and joy from his father. "I guess you're right," he said without much conviction.

"Better times will come, my son. Cheer up and drink your coffee before it gets cold," his father urged him.

"Give us Yab!" his father exclaimed, laughing at his own joke.

Although Yab felt slightly better after his dad's long story, he simply wanted to throw in the towel. In just a few short years, Yab had accumulated enough frustration and pain to last an entire lifetime. The political instability of the land hadn't been kind to him. Not only was the system unsupportive, but the circumstances seemed to be a threat to him and the ones he loved.

Three robberies in the past month, and those were a mere annoyance compared to what Yab had been through. Not long ago, a close family friend had been kidnapped for ransom. While his family negotiated for his release, his friend, Thomas, died as the ordeal had been too severe. Tears overwhelmed Yab's eyes at the thought of his close friend. This land had changed him. This land and all the bad people that tried to take advantage of good people like Yab and Thomas.

Thomas had been full of life, always wearing a smile. He was bigger than life, just like Yab's ideas. How many losses could a man endure in a lifetime, though? Especially at such a young age.

Yab couldn't handle the pressure. No matter how much he tried, he always ended up being a victim of corruption, losing friends and family in the process. If Manuel would've had a similar fate as Thomas, Yab would have never forgiven himself. Yab gritted his teeth and tried not to burst into a sobbing wail. How was he supposed to make anything good happen here?

His father quickly picked up on Yab's agitated state and tried to help with yet another story.

"Let me tell you one final Mayan story," his father said, putting down the cup of coffee. "Do you remember any other stories I've told you about the Mayans?"

"Dad, please..." Yab responded in a defeated whisper. "I remember *all* of them. I'm just not like them, Dad. Never was, never will be. Our life isn't theirs. I don't know why you keep bringing them up!"

"Well, you're a descendant of them, so you're as much a Mayan as they were," his father corrected him. "Do you think the Mayans built their empire by despairing at their first attempt? If that was the case, they wouldn't have been able to invent the mathematical concept of zero, the use of limestone for construction purposes, or their hieroglyphic system. In the same way, you can't expect to succeed on the first attempt, Yab!"

Yab thought about it for a moment. It was true. Their success and glory hadn't come easily. They'd fought droughts, wars, hardship, and immigration to build an empire comparable to today's modern economies. However, Yab's streak of bad luck had been going for almost three years now. The hardships had finally depleted his energy–his very will to fight.

Considering the backstory of his Mayan ancestors, Yab remembered how they migrated when the famine struck. Their land was no longer capable of providing them with what they needed to survive and succeed.

Yab toyed with an idea that had been stuck with him for quite a while now. His efforts here were devoid of meaning and hope, his attempts fruitless. No matter how long he strived for success, it seemed like the place he was living rejected this promise of abundance.

Yab grabbed his now-cold cup of coffee and took a sip. The taste was almost painful to the tongue. Yab spat it out as the bitterness of the drink took over his entire mouth.

"Ugh" Yab was embittered by the cold temperature. He stared at the cup and thought that this cup of coffee wasn't so different from his experiences in life so far. Having a cup of coffee should be pleasant–a longed-for moment–especially when enjoying it alongside a loved one. The aromas of a good cup alleviate your worries and draw you in to take a sip–to taste the experience and try to understand its complexity and beauty, compelling you to share it with others.

However, Yab felt that whenever he leaned in to take a sip in life, he received a bitter and cold experience, almost as if he had waited too long before leaning in, just like it happened with his coffee right now. Yab was tired of being dealt a cold and stale cup of coffee; he was ready for a breakthrough.

Yab knew only one place where he could succeed and make things change: a place he had heard a lot about, where dreams supposedly came true.

"I'm thinking of moving out of the country–a rebirth I guess, like the new planting season," Yab said. "This isn't the place for me. Not anymore."

His father nodded and smiled as if he'd been expecting it. "Where would you go?"

"The US," Yab said with confidence. "I've been thinking about it for a while now. My efforts there would be appreciated. I might be able to achieve something for myself! And if not, at least, people won't steal from me there…"

"Son, everything you need is right here," his father said. "Why do you want to chase such a wild dream? What if you fail there too?"

His father wasn't the pessimistic type. He was always encouraging, but sometimes, his concern and fear for his son's well-being bested him. It was only natural for a father.

"I can't stand the situation here," Yab insisted. "If my ideas were bad, I would accept the failure gracefully. But watching my ideas fall into the hands of the predatory government, being a victim of backstabbing and corrupt political games? I can't stand that!"

Yab stared at the sky with a smile forming on his lips, thinking optimistically of the potential lying beyond his home. His father said nothing, peacefully sipping his coffee.

"I know the next big disruptor is somewhere out there, perhaps as huge as the coffee industry, Dad," Yab said. "All I have to do is find it in an environment that doesn't try to smother my best attempts."

"I support you, no matter what, Yab. You know that," his father said. "I just want to point out that you're still too young, and your inexperience might make you think that a brighter future is only possible away from here. However, when you grow up, you'll understand that everything you ever needed was right here, even if it's not as fancy as discovering a brand new global product from scratch, like–what was it that you said? He thought for a moment...Oh, yes. Like coffee! "You're intelligent, and you always think big, but those things don't happen overnight. The coffee industry took generations to flourish. I just want you to be reasonable."

"Dad, they say that if you plan to make your dreams happen within a time–so short as your lifetime–you're dreaming too small. I'm okay with laying down the seed that could set the foundation and letting future generations culminate it and make it a reality," Yab said. "And if I fail...I'll come back here, admit I was wrong, and start working on the field like you always wanted me to."

"I don't want you to admit that you're wrong, and I don't want you frustrated here working for me and not learning much. Your restaurant does good, but these are dangerous times. It's very sad for this country to see its brightest minds leave, and unfortunately, it might be a good time to try to migrate," his father smiled nervously. "I want to support you, but I know that one day, you'll figure things out by yourself, regardless of where you are living; don't ever forget your roots. There is no evil that lasts a hundred years, and not everything is bad in these beautiful Mayan lands. I know that sooner or later, you'll be back and help many."

Yab hugged his father and retreated to his room where he would plan the trip to America. He had so many things to do and coordinate. Yab was terrified about the idea of leaving his home, his friends, and his family. His stomach was revolting just at the daunting idea, but he wouldn't back down—not after so many failures here. His mind was on fire. Ecstatic. He barely slept that night, thinking of the vast possibilities in the US and of the life he could build.

3

THE MAYAN SPINNER
(PART ONE)

Yab was packing his belongings. He had been up since early in the morning, making a list of the essential things he would need for the trip: a pair of extra shoes, as many sets of clothes as would fit in the bag–five at least–rations, dry food, and all the savings he had amassed over the years. This would have to be enough to get him started.

Sitting on his bed, going over the list of crossed-off items, Yab felt a pair of eyes staring at him from the doorstep. He turned slowly to see his mother's troubled face.

"Your father told me about your discussion yesterday," his mother said in a bitter tone.

His mother's eyes scanned the things spread across the floor, fell on Yab's list, and ended up meeting his eyes once again. She seemed calm but somewhat troubled.

"So it is true?" his mother said and rushed closer, wrapping her arms around him. "Are you sure this is a good idea, Hijo?" his mother asked, squeezing him tighter.

"I am, Mama, yes," Yab responded. "I haven't been thinking about anything else all night long. I don't think I have anything left for me here professionally. If I want to succeed, I have to go to the US."

His mother raised a bitter smile, "I remember when you were just a baby, Yab."

"Don't be afraid, all right?" Yab said, flashing a reassuring smile. "Everything will be okay. I promise to call you every day."

"I can't keep you from leaving," his mother said. "If you think that's the best thing to do, I will support you, and I know you will find what you're looking for over there, I'm certain of it. You're kind-hearted and smart. No one would pass up an opportunity to work with my little boy and your aura bestowing abundance to everyone!"

"But…" His mother frowned. "I can't pretend I'm not worried about your wellbeing. The trip is dangerous."

"I'll be all right, Mama," Yab said.

"Promise me you'll be careful, okay?"

"I will, yes. You have nothing to worry about," Yab said.

"Okay," his mother said. "Your word is all I need. Please, go visit your Abuelo before leaving, okay? He will be devastated if you go without his blessing."

Yab had forgotten about his Abuelo. It had been a while since the last time they spoke. This was the perfect excuse to visit his favorite Abuelo once again.

"He needs to give you his blessing before you leave," his mother continued. "I might not allow you to leave if your Abuelo says so."

Grandfathers were highly respected in their community, and if a grandpa was against a certain plan or strategy, many of the family members complied. His mother did not say that out of spite but out of respect for her father's wisdom. Yab knew that if Abuelo gave his blessing, there was nothing stopping Yab from embarking on the trip.

"I'll pay him a visit now."

Yab's Abuelo was a medical doctor and was considered a wise man, known across town for his boundless heart, always eager to serve and help those around him. If Abuelo blessed Yab's goal and aspiration, despite the dangers along the way, no one in the family would object. Not that his parents would ever object; they both were always affirming and supporting Yab to the best of their ability, and he thanked them for that. Yab only hoped Abuelo would see the importance of his dream as well. He needed his sanction to boost his confidence and carry him to the promised land.

Yab left his bag half-packed and took the road to his Abuelo's small ranch, in the town's outskirts.

Yab had forgotten how beautiful the scenery was. Every little detail took him back to the days of his youth when he spent entire summers on his Abuelo's farm.

Yab crossed the splendorous river. Among the rocks, he saw the remnants of the destroyed, one-lane bridge where he used to race his cousins, horseback riding. The bridge was no longer there after the storms grew vehement over the years, but the memories were still lying with him.

Yab reached the trail he knew by heart, going up the mountain, reaching high enough to appreciate the lush green valley. Soon enough, amidst the dense foliage, he caught a glimpse of the best sight in the valley: the view of the magnificent Copán Ruins.

Abuelo and Yab had spent countless hours in the ancient city of Copán, one of the classic jewels of the Mayan Civilization: a true treasure to humanity. Yab smiled and remembered the innumerable times he played with his cousins around the rising temples and enclosed courtyards, and the more serious, and educative outings with his Abuelo learning about Mayan archeology. Yab was still blown away by the astonishing accomplishments of his ancestors.

The road led him through the dense expanse of the rainforests, straight to Abuelo's third-generation hacienda: a rural house made of adobe with a beautiful clay tile roof, sitting in a peaceful, bright clearing with a wonderful view of the blue afternoon sky.

Abuelo, just like every day, was out in the yard, digging the soil, inspecting the plants. Another man, a familiar face, was by his side. The man talked to his grandfather with reverence and respect, listening closely to what his grandfather had to say.

"Just give it a try," Abuelo said to the man. "I'm sure you'll see the results by the end of the week."

"Thank you, doctor," the man bowed deeply, greeted Yab, and left with an excited smile.

"Yab!" Abuelo stood up, dusting off the excess of mud and soil from his hands. "Your mother called me."

"That's why I'm here," Yab said. "How are you, Abuelo? Who was this man?"

"Just a friend, asking for advice about his wife's health," his grandfather said, inviting Yab with a gesture. "Come. Do you want some cacao?"

"No, thank you," Yab said.

"You loved that when you were little," his grandfather said. "Do me the honor and have a cup with me."

"All right."

His Abuelo prepared two cups of hot cacao, and they sat in the cottage's enclosed yard, in two chairs–his Abuelo had made those over the summer, as he was a craftsman as much as he was a man of science–under the crisp shadow of a tree that covered the entire backyard, overlooking a few cows in the background.

"So, your mother told me you decided to leave for the US," said Abuelo. "A lot of young men and women are leaving these days. Do you remember Pedro? His children are leaving as well. Are you going to join a caravan?"

Yab nodded. "I think it's the safest way to travel there."

"Are you sure of that?" his Abuelo said. "Why have you decided to leave?"

"I don't know why," Yab said with uncertainty. " I feel like I have to do this. It just seems right. I don't think I can do much here–not anymore. I want to grow. I want to find new goals and pursue them!"

Abuelo smiled and shook his head, suggesting that he had someday felt the same way too.

"Do you know what I remembered just now?" his grandfather asked. "The Hieroglyphic Stairway! Do you remember it?"

"Of course! The park's guard couldn't get me off it," Yab said. "How many times did I try to climb those stairs? Must have been at least a thousand! But how is this relevant?"

"Well, those weren't just any stairs; the staircase is part of the royal history of Copán," his grandfather said.

"You told me that many times," Yab said, sharing a laugh with his grandfather.

"What you *don't* know is that many of Copán's crucial events were recorded in this stunning monument.

"What kind of events?" Yab asked.

"Decisive ones, related to the sixteen kings of the city, starting with Yax K'uk Moh at the bottom and ending with the death of the last ruler of the city, Eighteen Rabbit," his grandfather recounted. "In many cases, these kings' milestones were the conflicts they had to experience in life, in order to succeed as leaders and rulers."

"And what does that have to do with me?" Yab asked.

Abuelo had always been keen on riddles, always posing questions and never giving a straight answer. He was a teacher at heart, always leaving Yab wondering for days, pushing him to come up with the solution himself. That was not the case this time, as Abuelo proceeded to explain.

"You're just like those rulers, now," his grandfather said. "You have conflict to overcome in your life, much like the kings did, but it won't keep you down for long. Your energy and your creative mind will solve that conflict, and from chaos, there will come order again. Your dilemma now is like a slingshot. It pulls you back only to propel you beyond the stars! "Mayans would migrate for long periods all the way to Mexico and then come back to town. Your goal doesn't have to be permanent; you can take it as an exploration to learn and grow.

His grandfather made a short pause.

"I know you're nervous about this, but there's no way you can grow without conflict or problems. The slingshot can't throw the rock far away if we don't pull the strings all the way back. Even if it hurts."

"Does that mean that I have to deliberately find conflict?"

"No, no, my boy," said Abuelo, laughing. "But you do have to embrace the conflict when it comes, focus on solving it, and learn from the experience…because that's what will help you get outside your comfort zone and grow! We don't run from our problems; we stand our ground, and we face them head-on…like warriors!"

"I thought you were going to be angry at me for wanting to leave," Yab said.

"Angry? On the contrary; I'm proud! I want to help, anyway I can, and I will pray for your safety!" Abuelo said.

"Where I'm going, Abuelo, I don't think you can help," Yab said.

"Have some faith," Abuelo said and stood up. "I have taught you many things over the years, Yab. Now, as the foreigner that you will become in your journey, I have something very special I need to give you that will help you achieve your purpose and keep you safe!"

Abuelo went inside the house and returned with a small antique wooden chest, placing it on the table with reverence. The old chest screeched open, and a puff of dust made Yab sneeze. How old was that chest, and when was the last time it had been opened?

Abuelo presented Yab with something that looked like a fidget spinner; an ornament made out of elegant jade with a very sophisticated design: four different bright colors decorated the edges–yellow, blue, red, and brown–all engraved with Mayans symbols.

Yab quickly realized that what his Abuelo held in his hands was hundreds of years old. It was intricate and unique; only an original Mayan artisan could have crafted something so elegant and beautiful.

"Where did you find this, Abuelo?" Yab leaned closer, astonished by the well-preserved relic.

"Yab, our ancestors, the ancient Mayans, apart from their robust market of sundry goods, had a sophisticated trade system, involving short, moderate, and extended routes to other Mayan cities."

"I didn't know that," Yab said. "How could they always be so ahead of their time?"

"I will surprise you, even more, my boy. My sixteenth great-grandfather was a noble merchant, and legend claims that he even traded with the Aztecs in Mexico," Abuelo said with his deep, storytelling voice. "But you see, the routes were very dangerous, as you can imagine. Picture the wild animals, enemy tribes, and just the terrain itself, or getting lost in dense jungles. They were like warrior explorers, venturing off to new lands, just like you plan to do on your trip to the US."

Abuelo placed the spinner before him.

"It turns out, Yab, that before being approved as Official Mayan Traders, these explorers had to train their minds like the famous Mayan Holcan Warriors did. "Remember from our archeology trips to the ruins Yab, that the Holcans were very effective fighting forces? They were fit physically to run long distances, disciplined mentally to respect the Mayan Warrior Code, and impeccably dressed–with painted faces to be feared by the enemy" And this spinner"–Abuelo pointed at it–"was the graduation amulet given to Holcans and Mayan traders at the top of the Mayan temple where they would manifest their mantra/affirmation for the first time. The Mayan translation for the Spinner would be 'Holcan Warrior Exploration Code'. It secretly goes into your pocket so you can always have access to it and use its powers so it can never be lost or stolen. The spinner has been handed down the family through generations, from my sixteenth great grandfather, all the way to me. Your mother decided to stay here in Copán with me–that's why she never received the spinner–but you know that you're ready to leave your land, and I think it's time for you to have it…for as long as you need it before passing it on to someone else…"

"Abuelo…I don't know what to say," Yab said, looking at it from different angles to examine its shape and design.

"Put it in your pocket, Yab. Feel the different surfaces."

Yab obeyed and shoved it in his pocket, lightly tracing the different surfaces.

"I feel four different textures," Yab said. "I can only assume there's a different meaning attached to each circle, right?

"Very good. I can sense your enthusiasm!" Abuelo said and took the spinner back in his hand. "Everyone knows that the Mayan astronomers of Copán calculated the most precise solar calendar; an astonishing feat for their time and the most precise among the Mayan civilizations. What most people don't know is that all these symbols on the spinner were extracted from the calendar. They were more than just hieroglyphs. They were living principles!"

Yab inspected the symbols closer with anticipation, eager to learn the meaning behind each one.

"So, let's start with the yellow one here at the top. Do you know what it represents?" Abuelo asked.

"That's easy," Yab said. "It's the Sun."

"Yes, Yab, well done. The Mayan sun was of huge importance to the civilization for conferring life, for understanding the passage of seasons to prepare to farm, and for following eclipses specific to religious purposes!" Abuelo said with enthusiasm. "What do you think the sun represents in the spinner?"

Yab stared at the Yellow circle puzzled, "I don't know. I can't think of anything."

Abuelo smiled. "It represents your internal dialogue, symbolizing the power of your subconscious.

"What is the subconscious, Abuelo?"

"Think of it as a very large cloud drive that stores everything you think of but are not necessarily paying attention to, Yab." The truth as you know it and perceive it is stored in your subconscious mind.

Abuelo noticed Yab's contemplative gaze and decided to explain further.

"Put simply, internal dialogue is the conversation our self-esteem is having with itself," Abuelo explained. "The sun in the spinner protected Mayan traders' internal dialogue–that little voice that we all hear in our heads constantly working to maintain us in reality. For example, have you ever heard your little voice trying to put you down, Yab? Saying something like 'that object is too heavy; you won't be able to pick it up'…Telling you that you're going to hurt yourself…That's your subconscious having an internal dialogue with your conscious mind. If you carry the Spinner in your pocket, Yab, it will help you watch over the misrepresentations in your subconscious, which will help you make your best efforts to deal with any situation you need to overcome and resolve. It will help you realize that you are strong, Yab!

"These mental breaks from reality are called blind spots; and believe me, we all have them!"

"Why do we have them?" Yab asked. "How do they come to be?"

"They can be a consequence of bad personal experiences but not only that," Abuelo said. "Blind spots can also be a byproduct of faulty education; the ill motives of authority figures; the result of collective, erroneous societal beliefs; or even family members' biased teachings.

"So, the little voice in my head isn't always right? Yab asked.

"Exactly, Yab. Our minds can develop inaccurate beliefs that are not only wrong but also dangerous. Just recently, you went through three robberies. That's not easy, and I heard about your best friend blatantly stealing from you. That is certainly negative and will affect your judgment in the future. However, not every friend in your life will betray you, so watch your self-talk when your mind is revisiting this experience. Constantly expecting the worst of others will certainly lead you to unwanted paths," Abuelo said.

Yab nodded, beginning to realize what his Abuelo was trying to teach him.

Abuelo rested his hand on Yab's shoulder and squeezed lightly. "So, control your internal dialogue so that you can always stay optimistic and try to inspire and help others.

"I will try to stay confident with a growth mindset, Abuelo," Yab said.

Abuelo stared at Yab with a smile that reflected the deep feelings of pride he felt toward his grandson. "Yab, come inside I want to show you something special."

Yab followed his Abuelo into the house. The short Abuelo placed his arm around Yab and led him toward the living room.

Yab's memories of his youth returned to his mind. He remembered all the nights he spent here when he was still a boy, listening to his Abuelo's stories all night long, learning all sorts of things, from everyday lessons to family tales. Yab smiled at the idea of those nights. It was all so simple and innocent back then, and his meeting with Abuelo now reminded him of those days, alleviating the anxiety that had built up in his chest.

Abuelo stopped before a framed image and pointed at it. "Look at this image, Yab, and tell me what you see," Abuelo said.

Yab inspected the image closely, leaning forward to take a better look.

"I see an angry Mayan looking at himself in the mirror," Yab said, laughing.

"Look closer, Yab," Abuelo instructed. "Look beyond your first impression."

Yab did as his Abuelo instructed and squinted his eyes, trying to understand what the old man was trying to show him. After exhausting the details on the heads, Yab turned his attention to the darkness between them. Yab finally saw something. His Abuelo was already smiling. "I see a...vase? I think I see a vase between the faces!"

"Exactly, Yab! That's the point I was trying to make. Watch your internal dialogue with patience. Take into account all sides of a story before making a judgment or rushing to make a decision! Now that you have this image imprinted in your mind, even when you forget to check your internal dialogue, this image will help you to pay close attention to every detail and to every bit of information before you; remember this and your subconscious will seldom fool you."

Yab was beginning to understand what his Abuelo was trying to teach him. The idea of internal dialogue was pretty clear, but Yab still had no idea how to apply his Abuelo's teachings. "Abuelo, I'm still not sure how to *use* the internal dialogue to protect my bad thoughts," Yab said sincerely.

"It's not an easy concept," Abuelo said. "Let me give you a simpler example. We are far back in the past now, and I want you to imagine a Mayan trader in the middle of the jungle: lost, battered, a tropical storm lashing his face, forbidding him from following his usual trade route. What is this trader going to do? Like the Warrior he is trained to be, the trader must be very careful of what he thinks and does in order to survive. His internal dialogue must stay positive, for if he gives in to his subconscious misrepresentations or the bad influences accumulated from others, the outcome could be fatal. Therefore, the line of thought that will determine his decisions had better be intelligent, well-advised, and optimistic so he can successfully get back on his journey. What I'm trying to say is, be careful about misleading beliefs in your head created internally and externally. Who you surround yourself with and, more specifically, who you agree with, are key to being successful. Always be skeptical about the information received from others that you sanction in your mind!"

"I'm nervous, Abuelo. So much good information," said Yab, in awe. "Will you pray for me when I leave?" Yab asked.

"Oh, my sweet boy!" Abuelo exclaimed gently. "I pray for you every day and will keep on doing so until the day I die! And listen–if there's one thing you should remember from this conversation, it's that your subconscious responds based on your own idea of the truth and not according to the truth as it really is. So, be patient in every circumstance, and remember that every story has two sides before jumping to conclusions.

"Yes, Abuelo, I will," Yab said with confidence.

"Very well," Abuelo said. "Now, the second symbol, the dark blue, is the Mayan star!

Do you know why the stars are important, Yab?"

Yab shook his head.

"The stars and heavens have always guided every single one of us, and this stands true throughout many generations, up until today! Stars guide the farmers, the hunters, the fishermen, the warriors, and, of course, the migrants, and they will guide you in your journey too!"

"What do the stars symbolize?" Yab asked.

"Always getting ahead of yourself," Abuelo chuckled. "The stars are an inspiration to set lofty goals, trying to reach very high in your life, outside of your comfort zone, so you can do wonderful things for humanity."

Abuelo paused and his eyes lit up. "I have an idea," he said. "Will you do me the honor of sleeping here tonight as you used to do when you were little? That way we can look at your favorite stars at night–the ones that you kept pointing at when you were a kid."

"I think it was Venus, right?" Yab exclaimed.

"Ah, you always knew a lot about stars," Abuelo said, laughing. "Venus represented love in the Mayan times. No wonder your heart is full of love and filled with an insatiable desire to do good!"

Yab thought about it for a moment. He would be away for quite some time. It could be months or even years before he had another chance to relive his youth and spend some quality time with his grandfather.

"I will stay tonight," Yab said. "It's been a while since we did that together."

"You honor me, Yab," Abuelo said.

And so he did. Yab spent the day there and they postponed their conversation until the sky was dark, the moon full, and the stars peppering the black sky. It was a beautiful sight, so clear and imposing.

4

THE MAYAN SPINNER (PART TWO)

Yab and his Abuelo sat on the porch with two glasses of wine and they resumed their conversation, at last.

"Now," Abuelo said, "warriors and migrants always need clear objectives, and the stars remind us that there are endless possibilities to choose from and thus we need to focus."

Abuelo pointed at the thousands of tiny dots in the sky, his point clear before Yab's eyes. In order to choose a single star, he had to focus.

"Do not be afraid of the challenges ahead of you, as the key lies in thinking big and having vivid goals in your mind, Yab."

"I can see that," Yab said, staring at the sky, letting Abuelo's words sit with him in the peaceful nightly silence.

"The Mayans were keen observers of the skies. They believed that understanding the universe would allow them to comprehend the will of the gods and thus win favor from aligning their objectives with those of the gods," Abuelo said. "Now, in modern times, I believe we can still be inspired by this and find a practical way to apply it in our lives. Along your journey, try to find *your* stars, Yab, and relate them to your dreams and actions."

Yab tried to practice what his Abuelo said, attempting to single out Venus so he could allow its light to shine upon him. "I love how dark it gets here. It's easy to look at the stars here, an entire ocean of them. They make me think big and open my imagination!" Yab said.

They took a sip of their wine before continuing.

"That's why I asked you to stay tonight," Abuelo said. "When I was your age, for New Year's, I used to bring a piece of paper when observing the Stars, and I would jot down my goals. I felt like I could choose anything, among infinite options! I felt like a king observing the stars, and there was nothing to stop me from choosing what I wanted to do. After a prudent time, even if a goal failed, there were thousands and thousands of other goals I could still pursue! Always remember that, Yab. There's always another way. There's always a *better* way but, to be able to see that, you shouldn't limit yourself to what you already know. Look at the stars and lose yourself in their infinite vastness! It's what we could call *thinking big*!"

"I think I can do that, Abuelo," Yab said.

"Nowadays, all you kids do is type everything in your mobile phones," Abuelo said, giggling. "Nonetheless, it doesn't matter if it's a piece of paper or your mobile phone. Single out your favorite star–your goal–and write it down, and don't let it slip out of your focus!"

"That seems fairly easy," Yab said.

"Okay, so let's complicate things just a little," Abuelo said. "I could have told you about the stars this morning, but I wanted you to be here so that you could see them and experience them. When I'd pinpoint my goals, I would write down such colorful ideas that, later on, when I read them aloud, I could not only picture them in my mind but I could also feel them create an emotion in my heart!

"I later learned that this is because we, humans, think in three dimensions. We first think in words. Then, the words activate an image, which is our second dimension. The third dimension is accessed when we think in emotions, which awakens our hunger to grow and try new things like what you're experiencing right now."

"So, when you write your goals, make sure they are very vivid–enough to trigger an emotion, Yab. As vivid as the center circle of the spinner! Can you guess what that symbol is?" Abuelo showed him the engraved symbol in the middle.

"This is definitely a macaw, Abuelo," Yab said.

"Yes, Yab. Very good! The symbol of fire and passion for the Mayans," Abuelo said.

"What does that have to do with what we're talking about?"

"Your goals have to be like the macaws!" Abuelo said.

"What do you mean?" Yab asked, confused.

"Close your eyes," Abuelo suggested.

Yab closed his eyes.

"Do you remember what a macaw looks like?" Abuelo asked.

"Of course," Yab said. "Their colors are so rich, It's hard to forget." Once Yab responded without thinking, the realization came to him. He opened his eyes only to find Abuelo smiling.

"That's what your goals should be," Abuelo said. "Your goals should be vivid–as vivid as the image of the macaws in your head–and awaken the passion within you!"

"I think I understand," Yab said. "But how is that going to help?"

"Close your eyes again, and let me tell you a story," Abuelo said. "Do you remember the maltreated macaws on the fence at the ruins– the ones that after generations of people clipping their wings could no longer fly?"

Yab closed his eyes again, "Yes, of course. It was so sad to witness."

"When I was about your age, I had a goal that coincidently involved the macaws! I kept imagining how I wanted to see the flightless and extinct Macaws glide once again over the ruins and all of Copán Valley, just like they used to in the Mayan times. I dreamed about their colors, bright and shiny, flying above our houses. My soul was warm, and I was excited–full of passion! I told the elders of my time about it," his grandfather said in a trance-inducing voice.

"The people of my time thought I was crazy. They told me that the domesticated macaws would never learn to fly again, but I didn't give up. You see, my goal was so evocative, vivid, and relentless that it simply couldn't be brushed off by others. I slept and woke up with that image in my head. I kept thinking of their red feathers flapping above us, flying free, cawing with joy."

Guided by Abuelo's words, Yab was able to imagine the beautiful sight, the inviting colors of the birds drifting through the skies, adding dashes of vivid paint to the greenish backdrop with the skill of a master painter. Yab's heart was stirring.

"Now, open your eyes, Yab, and tell me what you see," his grandfather said.

Two beautiful macaws cawed, drifting in circles right above the house, and two more had perched over Abuelo's Copán Patio. It felt like magic. Yab rubbed his eyes and pinched his forearm to ensure that he wasn't dreaming. But the macaws were there, and they looked at him as if they knew more than he did. Yab had no words to describe what he was seeing, and his mouth hung open. Their colors were exactly as he envisioned them in his own imagination.

"It took me twenty-five years to achieve my goal, and now the macaws fly once again over the ruins because I never lost sight of my goal, I never forgot what my goal looked like. In my case, it was easy to make them vivid in my head because the macaws *were* my goal. But you have to do the same with your goals; when you close your eyes, you have to picture your goal clearly; the more details you can think of, the better. Your goal has to be an image you will never forget! They were a symbol of fire and passion to the Mayans, and I hope they will be a symbol for your goals as well; a symbol of stimulating imagination, boldness, and perseverance!"

"I can see that now, Abuelo," Yab said, still unable to believe the magic taking place before him. The macaws were still cawing above their heads.

Yab nodded slowly. It had been a while since the last time he felt such profound wisdom radiating from his grandfather. Looking back, it was always there, but Yab was only now mature enough to appreciate it.

"Abuelo, I think you forgot the fourth circle of the Spinner," Yab said.

"Oh no, Yab, I have not," Abuelo said, laughing at Yab's puzzled expression. "Because the fourth circle is so effective that it works on its own even if the other three haven't been activated. That is why it's a spinner! The fourth circle represents the Mayan warrior who will guard your creative mind!"

"What does the warrior represent?" Yab asked.

"The holcan warrior protected traders throughout the course of their long journeys, and the holcan warrior in you will also protect you, Yab. It will give you the energy you need to resolve conflict in every moment!" Abuelo exclaimed with sheer reverence to the warriors. "This is the force created by your new goals. It's your creative mind kicking in, and it will nurture your appetite to learn and be resourceful in solving problems. That's why I trust you can go on your journey because I can see your creative mind; the warrior within you is strong!"

"But how will I know how to achieve my goals?" Yab asked.

"That's the thing. You don't have to know how to achieve your goals. Just set your goals, clearly and vividly, and let your creative mind, with the help of God, figure it out and seize every opportunity!"

"So, I have to follow the sun and trust that it will illuminate my internal dialogue. I have to look through the unlimited options and focus on the specific goals that I'm passionate about so I can visualize them clearly and vividly as the Macaws, and then I have to let the creative mind, my inner warrior, do their work?" Yab asked. "Is it that simple?"

"It is," Abuelo said. "Now, let's head to bed, and tomorrow I'll let you in on the last secret that combines everything–how to activate the power of the spinner. It will be the secret ingredient that brings everything to life!"

And so they retired. Abuelo laid the bed for Yab and retreated to his room. Yab spent the night staring at the spinner and the stars out the window. Under the luminous night, Yab felt he had God's blessing and his Abuelo's wise gaze with him, always looking after him. Yab slept peacefully with the spinner in his hand and a warm smile on his lips.

The following day, his Abuelo woke him up with a cup of coffee. Yab thanked him for the beverage, along with all the wise words and the precious relic.

"Now, as I promised yesterday, I'll teach you the secret ingredient that puts everything together," Abuelo said.

Yab took an eager sip of hot coffee.

"Back in Mayan times, the merchant graduates gathered atop the temple for their culmination ceremony. This ritual was sacred and exclusive for warriors, executed carefully and with reverence as the Mayan Temples were the most sacred monuments for the Mayans."

"Yes, the kings lived there, correct?" Yab asked.

"Exactly. And when the kings died, they turned into gods, so it was believed that their spirits were guarded in these temples, so the ground was sacred, and this important ceremony took place there at a monument of utmost importance, in the heart of the Mayan Empire!"

"Well, we don't believe in that today, do we?" Yab asked.

"No, that's why I have my own parallel about where your graduation should take place. For us Catholics, there is an equivalent to the Mayan temples. It's our own bodies!"

"Our bodies?"

"In the New Testament, in Corinthians, it's explained how our bodies are temples of the Holy Spirit: 'Who is in us and Whom we have received from God.'"

"So, what is the process to graduation then? I still don't understand," Yab said.

Abuelo smiled, enjoying Yab's anticipation. "The secret to activating the power of the spinner is creating your own thematic mantra, like a prayer–no more like an affirmation, Yab! In the past, at graduation, the merchant nominee delivered his mantra to turn his spinner on. Nowadays, you have to do the same, except for the ceremonial temple part. In your case, to enable the spinner's powers, you have to look within yourself. Remember you're a temple yourself, of the Holy Spirit–and in your heart, you'll find an astounding mantra.

Yab still wasn't getting it.

"I want you to come up with a theme, Yab. A thematic affirmation that will become your mantra, and every time you manifest this statement from within your heart, you will be manifesting your faith in God and entrusting your goals to him, much like the traders did back in the day to their Mayan gods!"

"So…my Mantra reveals the objectives I'm passionate about and perhaps even connects me to my purpose in life–and I need to manifest it permanently to make the spinner work?" Yab asked.

"Yes, exactly; plus we have our temple right here," Abuelo said, touching his heart with his index finger. "All you have to do is recite your mantra through *your* temple, and everything will come together."

"I think I understand now," Yab said.

Remember that the Mayan Star will help you create something new today, and these goals are the key to igniting the spinner. I know you have it in you already, Yab. Give it a spin," Abuelo encouraged him.

Yab did as instructed and gave the spinner a spin.

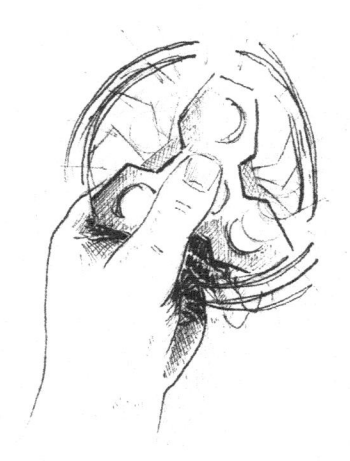

"See how all the colors blend with one another, becoming one?" Abuelo asked, and Yab nodded. "The spinning motion is the moment the mantra should be manifested in your head or out loud. See how you can't tell that they all are separate and of different colors? The mantra unifies the key elements and helps you become aware of your gifts and how you can help the world!"

"Abuelo, this is amazing," Yab exclaimed, staring at the fast, interchangeable colors.

"You see, sometimes, even with the macaws by our side, it might be easy to lose sight of our goals and lose our creativity amidst the confusion of the subconscious," Abuelo said. "My mantra always helped me stay focused. When I was in doubt, or when I lost sight, I recited my personal mantra, and I would have a clearer picture of what legacy I wanted to leave behind."

"So, I need to find my own mantra, essentially an affirmation of my goals, which are connected to my purpose?" Yab asked.

"Yes. Connecting your goals to your purpose will help you see clearly what it is that you are here to do. Without a mantra, the spinner will not turn; the same way that without goals, a purpose cannot be fulfilled."

"All this force will activate your creative mind! In my case, this was the mantra that helped me achieve my goal:

"I make people happy when they witness the fiery red, yellow, and blue macaws flying freely over Copán!"

"I always recited this mantra, and my passion never faded from my mind. You will make your own mantra, an affirmation that aligns with your goals–something that will make you feel warm inside when you repeat it in your head and make your goals as vivid as the macaws. Do you understand?"

"Yes, Abuelo, I think I understand what I have to do. I encourage my creative mind to be resourceful to resolve conflict and I need to trust that it will make me sharp and shrewd even if I have to learn something new. I need to guard my Internal Dialogue because if left unchecked, it can get negative, and that's who I will become. And finally, I need to have vivid goals in my head, as clear as the image of macaws. I need to affirm myself and those goals with my own mantra that will shape my future. Is that correct?"

Abuelo nodded with a proud smile, "That was all I had left to teach you, my boy, and I'm proud to pass the baton to a man greater than me."

"Thank you, Abuelo," Yab said with a bow of the head. "I can't thank you enough, and I want you to know how much I love you."

"Oh, my good boy!" Abuelo said, holding Yab's head. "I love you too, but if you wish to thank me, keep track of your journey's takeaways for me and share them when you visit me in the future, will you?

"And Yab, I want you to remember something," Abuelo emptied his cup of coffee. "No matter what happens, I will always be proud of you. Your journey will not be easy, and yet, it will give you the energy you want: great empowering energy for you to figure out who you want to be and to make the right decisions based on the goals you choose to work toward."

Such was his honor and awe, Yab fell into silence. He couldn't think of the words to express his immense gratitude. Yab only nodded with reverence.

"Make us all proud, make your goals come true, and provide abundance to many. Moreover, never forget your Abuelo when you become famous and successful!"

Yab felt ten feet taller after Abuelo's speech and waved goodbye with a brilliant smile. He was already starting to check on his internal dialogue, making an effort to make it better; his eyes narrowed on his goal, picturing it vividly as the macaws. Yab was ready to embark on his journey to the US.

He made his walk through the forest and stopped by the ruins, thinking about his mantra. *What should it be?* Yab thought. Just as his Abuelo taught him, he tried to picture his goals as clearly as possible. He imagined himself creating abundance for many small farmers. Perhaps they could grow chili peppers, spices, and plant-based foods. He saw families and friends working together and exporting their harvest globally, similarly to how he knew that his ancestors commercially dealt with coffee; he smiled as he envisioned the productive fields unfolding before him. But, how could he make this happen? Suddenly, the following affirmation came to Yab's mind:

My heritage and family values guard me and will take me and my goals into a brighter future!

With this newfound mantra, he would make his Abuelo happy and would work on improving it!

5

THE CARAVAN TO THE US

Yab was excited to embark on his trip to the US. His legs were cold with anxious excitement, his smile unfading. It would be the first step toward a new future. Many friends and some of his cousins had already decided to start afresh in the promised land, away from the adversities of their old lives. Yab's heart stirred at the thought of joining them and reinventing his life.

At the crack of dawn, Yab bid farewell to his family and told them not to worry about him. Once he was successful, he would return, and they would enjoy the ripe fruit of his efforts together. His father bestowed a confident nod and a smile, and his mother begged him to take care of himself. Yab reassured them that everything would work out and left to join the caravan.

Yab was outside of Copán, walking with his backpack tightly strapped around his shoulders, eager to meet his co-travelers. Yab stood at the side of the long highway leading outside of Copán and took a long look at the towering mountains gleaming under the sun and the expanses of grass that coated the land in its entirety. In the distance, his Abuelo's humble home stood atop a small hill, visible even from this far. Yab smiled and waved at his Abuelo, even though he wouldn't have been able to see him.

Yab turned his eyes to the road and saw a huge crowd of people in the distance. At least four hundred had already gathered as if for church services. They had all gathered under a massive tree, whose branches reached for the sky, spreading high above them like a canopy, offering its crisp shadow, and a comfortable place for respite for those who had already traveled for days.

Every time Yab and his father drove past this point, his father would always turn and point toward the tree.

"Remember, that's a ceiba tree," his father told him. "It was the sacred tree for the Mayans, holding the family creed. Isn't it imposing? Look at its colors…the gnarly bark. It's almost perfect!"

"It's very beautiful, dad," Yab always reassured his father, but he had never really paid close attention to the tree–not until now.

Much like the Abuelo's planting seeds blessed by the Ancestors, Yab wished the ceiba Tree could bless his journey.

Yab joined the caravan at the Guatemalan border and followed the people toward Mexico, much like his trader ancestors did hundreds of years ago.

He joined the caravan at the Guatemalan border and followed the people toward Mexico, much like his trader ancestors did hundreds of years ago. With his bag–full of sundries, rations, and money he could use in the US–Yab left his land with one final glance. It would be a while before he would see his family, friends, and the endless green of Copán. The Mayan merchants would have felt the same way, a bittersweet parting sensation within them.

Yab was excited to meet new people like him–eager for a better future. He looked forward to discussing with them, exchanging opinions and aspirations, and even working together toward their joint future. Yet, reality was much harsher than Yab had anticipated.

Entire villages of hopeful souls came together in a massive procession. Most had already traveled for a few days, already worn out and battered. No one looked hopeful. No one looked eager. Their eyes were bloodshot and their steps heavy with the onus of their choice. The entire procession was devoid of happiness, and soon enough, Yab's smile faded as well.

Their journey took them through torrid climates during the day and through rain and insufferable cold during the night. Yab's legs were burning, his forehead sweating, and his bones aching. Everyone's minds were dizzy and their mouths were dry.

Yab was one of the few with extra rations, clean clothes, water, and enough money to buy the things he needed during every stop. The other co-travelers looked at him with awe, craving what he had, even though it was just the essentials. It was a luxury to have enough water and food to last between stops. It was a privilege to have shoes to walk over the scalding asphalt. It was even a blessing to have a bag to store all that.

Pressed against one another, barely able to breathe in the choking heat, with barely enough space to walk freely and hundreds of hours before they would reach their destination, they only had each other's company and stories to pass the time.

Many people approached Yab, either to share their stories, to talk and alleviate the weight off their chests, or to simply pass the time with anecdotes, life lessons, and jokes. Yab quickly realized that not all of the people approaching him had good intentions. Some, after a few brief minutes of conversation, demanded Yab's food and water. He really didn't have a choice but to share his ever-scarcer resources. They were the same people that had ruined their lives back home and embarked on the trip to reshape a new one in the US. Unlike their other fellow travelers, these people were part of the problem they were running away from; bad people that only wanted to unjustly profit from others. The most upsetting part was that, had they not demanded things like that, Yab would have still gladly shared his surplus of food and water with them.

His Abuelo's words rang true once again. He needed to guard his internal dialogue against those who blamed others–from those who only cared for his "wealth," and from those who had done despicable things under the pretense that it was for their own survival. Yab held the spinner as his Abuelo had taught him, feeling the texture of the sun. He sought the sun's help to protect him from the bad and reveal to him those worthy of his time and companionship. Yab came up with a new affirmation:

"I always double-check what I sanction as true, so I am very careful to only agree with those who make me a better person."

Yab guarded his internal dialogue and managed to avoid those meaning him harm. He instead took notice of the (more than a few) kind parties within the unruly parade of suffering souls.

Compassionate and caring as he was, Yab took genuine interest in others' stories, absorbing all the experiences they had to share. They had gone through nightmarish situations and horrid events, and yet some were still smiling. They were all fighters in their souls, and Yab found that inspiring above everything else. "My wife and children are back home in Guatemala, but I left to raise money for them," a man said.

Without proper economic growth, the father of two was forced to seek a source of income away from his loved ones.

"I didn't want to leave," the man said. "I love my home. I love Guatemala, but I had no other choice."

"These are my two angels. I was the owner of a thriving business, but it wasn't good enough to raise them properly…" The woman pointed at two twin siblings, a boy and a girl, walking a few feet ahead of them.

"Why did you leave?" Yab asked.

"Our neighborhood was full of gangs," the woman said. "I was too afraid to leave and return home even in broad daylight. I'd rather die before letting these two become victims or even members of these gangs."

The woman had no money to move to a new apartment or move her business to a better location. She amassed her courage and left, forcing the children through this ordeal.

Among the business owners and the labor workers, there were a lot of farmers, eager to talk to Yab when they learned about his father's work in the coffee industry.

"The world is changing," a farmer told Yab. "I remember times when rain was enough to water the plants, the livestock, and we even begged for the rain to stop. Now, the rain is scarce and the plants wither and die. Your father definitely knows that!"

"He does, yes," Yab said. "It was a tough year."

"And I don't know anything else other than farming. That's what my father did, and that's what I hoped my sons would do, but not anymore. So, I just hope that where we're headed, they're in need of good, honest working hands…"

The most harrowing sight of all was the bulk of orphans in the caravan. From young children to teenagers acting as guardians for their siblings, they all hoped for a chance to see their parents that had migrated long ago and never returned.

Yab realized that he was one of the truly fortunate ones. His problems couldn't compare to the experiences of those around him. His restaurant was profitable, and his family had enough to last through many hardships. The people around him had nothing, forced out of their own lands, lands they didn't want to forsake, just for a shot at a normal life.

Yab had never thought about all that. His eyes opened to the new, cold reality. The crudeness of people's stories shocked him. The motives for migrating were aplenty, and they all surpassed Yab's wildest speculations. There was a part of Yab that felt everyone was like him, migrating for success–to learn. Yab smiled bitterly at the irony before him: He had to leave his land to realize all the problems he always sensed existed but never could do anything about.

On one hand, he felt almost inspired, thankful for being there amongst the people of shattered homes and lost hope. He had learned more in a few days than in his entire life. Yab left, after all, to learn, and grow, and that he had been ever since joining the caravan.

On the other hand, Yab felt a surge of negative emotions overshadowing the blessing of growth, his heart aching, bitter with guilt. For all those days, Yab had extra resources to offer and he never did. Was that the way he wanted to live? Then again, he wasn't rich; he only had enough money to last through the journey and his arrival to the US. But, even so, he couldn't stand with his arms crossed amidst the harsh reality that he was bearing witness to.

The following day, during the early hours of the morning, as the heat rose and the asphalt burned, Yab took a good look at all the people around him: A couple of orphan boys walked barefoot on the boiling street; There were others who could barely stand after a few foodless and waterless days–saving their money for when they needed it most; others panted and wheezed, unable to walk any further.

Upon their first stop, Yab entered the mall on the side of the road and withdrew from his savings. He bought two pairs of shoes for the orphans and enough food and water for as many people as he could. They all looked surprised–aghast. Their smiles were warm and their words of appreciation were sincere.

They all sat together. For the first time, the people didn't retell old, harrowing stories. Instead, they shared lighter, more beautiful ones; things they loved about their homes and how much they would miss them. Yab had a frugal dinner that day, but the smiles of the other immigrants were enough to fill him up.

The journey lasted for another three nightmarish months. Three months on the road through hardships and ordeals no person should go through: from injuries to starvation and even death. For three months, Yab expended his savings, hoping to at least help those around him. If they made it to the US, they could start their lives over, but they had to get there first.

In those three months, Yab made a promise to himself: He would work hard, and he would become successful to help other immigrants like these. When he became rich, he would always remember the caravan and would always make sure to spare some of his money for his brothers and sisters, and this thought kept Yab company during the cold nights. Eventually, Yab came to a realization. "Success for me is not enough; helping these people warms my heart. From now on I'll strive, not only for me but for them also." Yab held on to this thought tightly. *Abuelo would be proud of it*, he thought, smiling. And after three months, the border finally loomed in the distance, bright, imposing, calling for them with whispers of success and the promise of a new future. They were almost there–almost free.

The things he learned through the trip were bitter and hard to swallow. The people traveling to the US were not grand dreamers. They were troubled souls, leaving their old lives for new ones, with the hope things would be better beyond the border. Despite their broken hearts, their hopes and dreams were vivid–much like the macaws. Yab could see them flying overhead and into the distance. They all followed the macaws into the unknown and hoped for the best.

Yab picked another goal from the star-filled sky and held the image in his mind, vivid and bright like the macaws.

"I let my fire and passion show through my hard work. I will succeed and then serve others as part of the process, helping them overcome poverty!"

His journey in the US was about to begin.

6

VICTOR'S DINER

Yab was the last person in the frugal waiting room, sitting at an uncomfortable chair that proved to be a curse for his already sore back. His foot tapped on the tile floor as he anxiously waited for the restaurant owner to call him inside for his interview. Yab suspected that it wouldn't be an easy process. There were five people–all immigrants–before him, but they all left with hung heads, dragging their feet out of the restaurant.

His head leaned back and touched the wall, his heavy eyelids closing. Yab didn't have a proper chance to rest. Once he arrived in the US, he spent a full day sleeping and quickly went job-hunting, a task that proved more challenging than expected. With the promise of the American Dream, Yab always thought that jobs were abundant in the

US. He always thought that people could easily shape their futures here. And yet, reality was much harsher.

Victor's restaurant was the seventh one Yab had visited today. The past week, he went through dozens of interviews, which all ended in rejection; some didn't want to hire an "illegal alien"–as they called him; others had too many applications and only a few positions to fill, accepting only those who'd work for close to nothing.

Yab was frustrated. The grand splendor he'd heard about the US boasting didn't seem to be a reality. Jobs didn't exist in abundance, and they didn't pay much either.

The most soul-crushing aspect of it all was that Yab had to compete against his compatriots for the jobs. Immigrants didn't take the jobs of the US citizens; they competed for jobs against each other.

The door to the owner's office slammed open. An applicant rushed out the door with tears in his eyes, sniffing and wiping them with the back of his hand, murmuring a series of incomprehensible self-loathing curses between tremulous lips.

Did Yab make a mistake in coming here? His funds were draining, and if he didn't land a job soon enough, he would have to return home.

"Mister Pineda," the owner called from the small office.

Yab straightened his back, spread his shoulders, lifted his chin, and wore his warmest smile before entering the unkempt office, finding the owner behind a desk heavy with paper stacks and binders–probably the other applicants' resumes.

The owner was a man of Eastern European descent with exaggerated characteristics and thinning silver hair. He rubbed his day-old stubble, looking at a piece of paper.

"Please, take a seat," the owner said in perfect English. "Nice to meet you, Mr. Pineda. I'm Victor."

"You can call me Yab," he said and they exchanged a brief handshake.

Victor seemed as tired as Yab. Judging by the bulk of resumes, Victor had already met with dozens of applicants before him. Victor's eyes skimmed through Yab's resume slowly.

"You were a cook back in Honduras?" Victor asked.

"A chef," Yab corrected him.

"Cook, chef, it's the same thing," Victor said. "If you can make good meals, that's all that matters, right?"

Yab didn't want to correct him again, and Victor made a good point, so Yab only nodded and smiled.

"So, I need a cook," Victor said. "My last cook was deported, you see, and the post has been open ever since. I can't cook, so I need one effective immediately."

"I'd also like to start working right away," Yab said.

"It's tough out there, huh?" Victor said, nodding somberly.

"You have no idea," Yab said.

"Oh, I do," Victor said. "Anyway, can you cook meat? The other guy served the best steak in the entire area!"

"Of course," Yab said. "Steak, burger, anything you need!"

"Good to hear," Victor said. "You see, the other guys before you–they didn't know how to crack an egg. I have a name to uphold, you understand?"

"Absolutely," Yab said.

"Okay." Victor clapped his hands. "I do this with all my potential cooks. I want you to cook something for me, okay? Come this way."

Victor showed Yab to the kitchen, which was stuffed with an excess of pots and pans and sorely lacking proper ovens and stoves. *This will be a challenge,* Yab thought.

"You see, the only problem is that the little stock there was left has been used up by the other candidates. See what you can find and surprise me, all right?" Victor said.

Despite being well-versed and adept within a kitchen, Yab had never been so desperate for a job. Inspecting the pantry, Yab felt the pressure building up. He had to make this opportunity count.

Yab went around the kitchen, picking the cutlery he could use, taking mental notes of the available ingredients, and getting a sense of the kitchen. Victor looked closely, inspecting every gesture Yab made.

The pantry was frugal with no meat, a few eggs, and to his surprise, some plant-based flour that had seemingly been there for quite some time. Yab couldn't make much with the few options in the pantry. Either he would have to tell Victor that and risk not getting the job or cook, fail, and lose the job anyway. Yab decided not to give up. He would have to improvise.

Yab picked the ingredients (a can of jackfruit, soy sauce, chili peppers, beans, cassava flour, onions, withered parsley, and garlic) and set them properly on the counter, dividing everything into piles based on the steps he'd need to follow. Victor seemed interested in Yab's meticulous process, leaning closer.

Yab held the spinner, feeling the texture of the middle circle between his fingertips, thinking about his goal vividly. He wanted the job. He *needed* the job. Yab asked the warrior to unlock his creative mind to become resourceful.

"I let my fire and passion show through my best work. I trust the warrior inside me. I trust my creative mind."

Yab thought and envisioned a delicious extra-crispy plant-based chicken patty within a warm, fragrant burger–as vivid as the macaws. It was steaming hot, gently dressed with salad, along with his signature sauce of alluring colors.

Even though Yab's specialty was chicken dishes, spices, and sauces, he had read a lot about the plant-based cuisine and had already found a way to create the plant-based chicken nuggets. He wasn't as adept with it as with other culinary techniques, but he could rely on his experience and knowledge of ingredients. Letting his creative mind lead him, with his goal firmly in his mind, Yab got to work.

Many believed that nothing could substitute for meat. Yab disagreed and had read it would eventually be made in labs. The beauty of the plant-based kitchen was in the binding of the spices, proteins, natural gums, and starches, which he could make on his own from potatoes and oats. With the right dosage and accurate handling, even a home cook could provide nearly indistinguishable results. Yab began studying plant-based cuisine to constantly improve his acclaimed plant-based chicken nuggets. The real challenge in this new food category was to invent the healthiest plant-based food combinations to support energy, mental clarity, and longevity. Even though he was still a student, Yab's goal was to impress Victor with this alternative dish and know-how while keeping true to his health-and-wellness values.

Yab spent almost an hour working without catching a breath. Multiple pots were boiling, and the pans were already burning. He made everything from scratch, even the mayonnaise and the buns. Yab had to show his best work in order to impress Victor. It was hard work–the work of a man in search of the American Dream.

Victor remained silent the entire time, simply investigating the process, revealing nothing of his true thoughts. Yab finally put together the burger, coating everything with his signature sauce–a sauce he had painstakingly crafted over the years after many trials and errors to use in his former restaurant–and presented the dish to Victor. His mouth open in surprise, Victor stuttered, unable to express his feelings. He leaned and looked at the burger from every possible angle.

"It looks exactly like a chicken burger!" Victor said and grabbed it in his hands.

He took a bite, and closed his eyes, chewing slowly.

"It even tastes like one, and it's deliciously spicy–almost cajun!" Victor exclaimed. "You didn't use any meat! How did you do that?"

"It's the combination of the spices and chilies with the appropriate color and texture," Yab said humbly. "Even chicken itself wouldn't taste that good without my secret sauce."

"It's not like a real country fried steak, but I love it! Bet we could use that delicious sauce with a steak as well!" Victor took another bite. "I can't express how tasty this is!"

In four quick bites, Victor devoured the entire burger and leaned back in his chair. Yab waited patiently for the verdict. Victor liked his burger, but his judgment was still pending.

"Look," Victor said. "We cook steak, fries, and eggs here–American stuff, you know."

"I know," Yab said. "But I didn't have anything else available."

"I expected an egg and some fries," Victor said in disbelief. "Not this…"

Yab kept staring at Victor, saying nothing, awaiting the final response.

Victor finally smiled. "You are hired!" Victor exclaimed.

Yab felt like breathing again and fought the tears welling up his eyes. After so much hard work, his efforts were finally being rewarded.

"We could improve the menu together," Victor said. "You're clearly overqualified for this job, Yab, but hey…lucky me, right?"

"I'd like to work on the menu, and I need the job, so…" Yab said with a wide smile.

"Can you start tomorrow?" Mr. Victor asked.

"I can start today!," Yab said.

"Go home and celebrate. I'll see you tomorrow, okay?" Victor extended his hand for a quick shake. "You let me know what you'll need for the pantry, and I'll stock it tomorrow first thing in the morning!"

Yab prepared a list for Victor and left the store with his spirit uplifted, humming an old song his mother used to sing while cooking for him and his father. It was true after all. If you worked hard and let your passion show through your best work, you could achieve anything.

7

THE SHELTER

The foundation had been laid, a layer of economic security and comfort alleviating the stress, and Yab's future began getting clearer: he would work hard, save up a few extra bucks, and one day he could start his own business, like the one he had back home, only without the daily insecurity, caused by the high levels of socio-economic inequality and political turmoil.

Yab found himself with enough time on his hands now that he didn't have to go around town looking for a job. Not knowing what to do with the free time, Yab decided to take a tour on his own and do some sightseeing.

His short stroll around town took him to a colorful taco restaurant. Yab was already hungry, and the restaurant's fragrances reminded him of Central America's local cuisine. Yab couldn't resist paying a visit and having a taste of home after days of eating junk food.

Inside the shop, Yab saw an old immigrant couple, the owners, sitting behind the counter with just a few customers inside. Yab saw them talking indistinctly. Yab couldn't hear what they said, but their faces revealed the whole story. Judging by the few ingredients available behind the counter and the few people idly eating inside, the restaurant wasn't a smashing hit.

When Yab approached the counter, the woman greeted him as her husband prepared a tray of tacos and placed them in a takeaway bag.

"I'll drop those by the shelter," the husband said.

"Excuse me," Yab said. "What type of shelter? Sorry to interrupt!"

"There's an immigrant orphans' shelter down the street," the husband said.

"We try to offer some of our tacos to the children because the food there is atrocious," the woman said.

Yab remembered the orphans in the caravan. What if some of those orphans ended up in this shelter? Now that he had a job secured, it would be a good idea to pay a visit and see if there was a way to make their lives easier, Yab decided.

"Could I come with you?" Yab asked. "It's been a week since I've been here...I know what some of these kids have gone through."

The husband gave Yab a gracious half-smile. He and his wife had probably gone through the same process that Yab was talking about.

"All right," the man said. "You can carry the tacos for me."

"Of course!"

Yab's enthusiasm about going to the shelter quelled his hunger in no time. On the way to the shelter, the man told Yab about all the problems they had encountered since they opened up the shop: Overwhelming city permits and fees, increased competition leading to fewer and fewer customers every year, and some months ending up in debt.

"I wish we had never left," the man said. "It was all simpler back in Mexico."

They arrived at the shelter, and Yab's face lit up; he immediately recognized a few familiar faces from the caravan. The kids were playing basketball, hide and seek, or lounging on the wooden benches and talking. First came a surge of cold shock; those children never made their way to their parents. They were stuck here, waiting for the days to go by until they would eventually be deported or let loose in the streets. Then came joy. It was nice to see the familiar faces again, and Yab was here to help.

"The tacos are here!" A child exclaimed, and all the children rushed in their direction.

Among the familiar faces, Yab saw the barefoot boys–now wearing shoes–staring at him.

"So glad to see you are okay!" Yab said and hugged them tightly in his arms.

The drab atmosphere became joyous, almost festive. Yab and the children quickly bonded and talked about their experiences so far in the US. They were all together in this, a community of expatriate dreamers, longing for each other's company and support.

"I know it might seem hard now, but it will get better," Yab said to the circle of children around him.

"How do you know that?" one of the barefoot children asked.

"I have been through many ups and downs myself," Yab said. "I know you're still young and you have to live here, away from home; but you have each other, and if you have faith, you can achieve anything!"

Some of the children shared their dreams, their ideal jobs, and goals. One wanted to be a chef like Yab; another wanted to be a policeman like his father, and a few wanted to be musicians or Hollywood actors. They were still young, and their minds were wild and vibrant with seemingly crazy ideas, but Yab didn't dishearten them. Instead, he chose to share the little secret he recently found.

From his pocket, Yab pulled the spinner and explained the meaning of every circle and every symbol, finally explaining the importance of a mantra.

"If you affirm yourself with your thematic mantra, you will manifest this power," Yab said. "And trust me, you can achieve anything you put your minds into!"

The children seemed impressed, taking a good long look at the spinner.

"Where can we get one of those?" a kid asked.

"You don't need one," Yab said. "Remember that your temples are your own bodies! All you have to do is enchant your hearts! Having a spinner helps, but you don't need one in order to apply its wisdom!"

Yab spoke to them as if they were his own kids, the same way his Abuelo and his parents encouraged him all those years.

When the night came, one of the shelter volunteers came out to the yard. "Dinner time!"

A series of displeased murmurs spread across the crowd of children.

"Isn't any food good here?" Yab asked a boy.

The boy shook his head. "I only like tacos."

How bad could the food be?

They entered the dining area, and Yab's smile vanished. There was a big pot of lentil soup at the far end, and when Yab took a bowl and tasted it, he grimaced. *Too salty, over-boiled, and drowned in sunflower oil*. Watching the children idly fiddle with their soup, wincing with every spoonful of lentils, Yab decided to talk to the volunteers.

"Excuse me," Yab said politely. "Do you cook your own meals?"

"No, we have a catering company," the woman said. "It's not good, I know, but we can't afford anything else."

"I see," Yab said, simply staring at the children, who despite being hungry, could barely touch their bowls.

Yab thought about it. His free time would be scarce and limited, and he could use that time to improve himself and achieve his goals. But the kids deserved something better than this tasteless lentil soup. Who offers lentil soup to children anyway?

"What does it take to be a volunteer here?" Yab asked.

"Nothing really," the woman said. "Just enough enthusiasm to help and provide. Are you interested?"

"I can't commit full time, but I would like to drop by occasionally and cook for them," Yab said. "I'm a chef, and I could do something better than this, for less money than what you are paying probably."

The woman's eyes lit up.

"Of course! It would be an honor. We don't have many volunteers here, so we'd appreciate the help. And the children will love a proper meal!"

"I won't let you down," Yab said.

As promised, a week later, on his first day off from work, Yab returned to the shelter with two bags full of groceries, with an entire menu planned out in his mind. Unlike the catering service that dropped off the food and left, Yab wanted to cook with the children and the other volunteers. He could teach them the recipes, laugh, and cook together. It would be a bonding experience–one that would hopefully remind them of the time they spent with their families back home.

Yab visited the shelter's shabby kitchen and prepared the ingredients. It wasn't much, but it would be just fine for the simple dishes they would create. They cooked paellas and tacos together, along with his healthy plant-based chicken nuggets: A cheap, delicious alternative and easy to make. The fact that Dominic had stolen the possibility for him to make money off it didn't affect his ability to cook it freely for a noble cause. The children cheered as Yab and the volunteers served the proper dinner and ate with satisfied smiles.

Yab stayed up late, past their bedtime, to clean up the kitchen and the dining hall when the volunteer woman returned and asked Yab to visit them more often. The ingredients would be paid for, of course, and Yab could offer them a taste of home.

Yab accepted, "Anything for the little ones…I know what they've been through. It's the least I could do."

Yab returned home that night feeling lighter–at ease and at peace. They had gone through a lot, but he was in a position to help now, and he would use that chance to offer them a better life here. Yab wished there were more ways in which he could help. He would stick with the dinners for now, and when he became successful, he would never forget about the children there. Yab fell asleep while reciting his mantra, allowing his internal dialogue, his passion, his goals, and creative mind to become one, working together toward fulfilling his purpose in life. Yab repeated his mantra, time and time again, and his vision became clearer: A stable well-paying job, paying job so he could visit the orphans and help them out any way he could. That became a part of his vision now.

My best work brings personal stability, which allows me to use my talents to change lives and influence the less fortunate.

8

TASTES LIKE THE REAL DEAL

Life in the US wasn't easy. Yab had a stable job and, thankfully, Victor always paid on time. And yet, Yab barely made enough to live. With only a year under Victor's employment, Yab couldn't ask for a raise, and with the few spare hours Yab had at his disposal, he either studied a few culinary books he managed to buy, or he spent his time at the shelter, cooking for the orphans.

His apartment was downtown in a not-so-friendly neighborhood. At night, only the police car sirens echoed in the streets, which didn't instill much comfort. While he could afford an apartment in a better area, no one would lease him a house due to his immigration status.

Yab had to settle for the faulty apartment with the broken radiators and inconsistent plumbing for now.

Yab tried to remain positive through the daily ordeals, nonetheless. It was all a small stepping stone toward success. When his mind began to stray away, Yab would hold the spinner in his hand and repeat his mantra.

He tried to guard his subconscious against the negative experiences. That wasn't the American Dream. That was just the beginning, and everyone had to go through it. Yab prayed to God and affirmed himself, shielding his mind from the negative experiences. It kept him centered and focused. It was all part of the plan. At least, that's what Yab kept telling himself.

After a long shift, Yab was in the kitchen, scrubbing the fat residue from the pan. Normally, it wasn't a cook's job to clean the entire kitchen. Yet, Yab was the chef, the cook, and the cleaner in this scenario. Yab scrubbed harder, letting the frustration materialize and convert into drive.

It took one good hour to clean everything up–an unpaid extra hour, of course–before Yab had finished his shift and dropped into a chair, sighing in relief. Another long day was over.

Yab didn't complain about all the extra hours he had to work. His shifts grew progressively longer, serving more customers throughout the day–and cooking more food. When the janitor had to move upstate for a better job and the waiter was deported, Yab's assignments expanded from just cooking to cleaning, polishing, and serving the customers. But the salary remained the same.

Victor had promised to hire new employees to help Yab out. A whole month went by, and no new employees showed up, though.

The steppingstone grew in size. "Just a little longer", Yab kept telling himself.

"Just bear with me," Victor said. "I'm still looking for a replacement."

Victor never hired anyone else. No matter how kind he was, the restaurant was always his first priority. More than once, Yab caught Victor sighing in desperation, going through the mountain of bills piling on his desk. Yab knew the position that Victor was in and stopped expecting someone to show up or for a raise to come. Yab and Victor weren't that different. In order to save the restaurant, Victor would do anything, and Yab would have probably done the same in his shoes. Yab respected that, and that's why he stuck around even though there were better-paying jobs out there. Yab preferred to work for someone who genuinely cared rather than spending his valuable time helping a horrible boss. Yab only hoped that Victor could see that too.

"Yab," Victor called from his office. "The last customers left. Clean up and go home, okay?"

"Okay, Mr. Victor," Yab said, putting the last of the pans on the piles with the freshly washed cutlery.

"You have the keys I gave you, right?" Victor said.

"I do, yes," Yab said.

"Good, good," Victor said. "Lock the place up and don't forget to get the kitchen light this time. I don't want to be paying the electric company a dime more than necessary! Oh, and take home anything you want to eat. I have to go. A couple of friends are waiting for me."

Victor rushed out the main door, leaving Yab alone, with only the plinks of the faucet disturbing the silence. Yab cleaned up the last of the plates the customers had left behind, stacking them on the large tray lying on the table.

Yab leaned against the counter, closing his eyes for just a moment, thinking of how warm and comforting his bed would be. Then, he took a deep breath, determined to clean up the kitchen and head home.

As he turned on the faucet, the restaurant's bell rang in the distance.

"Did you forget something, Mr. Victor?" Yab called out from the kitchen.

A faint murmur came as a response.

Yab stepped out of the kitchen only to find a young couple standing awkwardly by the door.

"Are you still open?" the girl asked.

"I'm sorry," Yab said, furnishing a tired smile. "I'm closing up."

"Where should we go now?" the boy asked in a whisper.

Yab thought about it for a moment. Yab wanted nothing more than to head home and catch some rest, but he wasn't the type of chef to leave two hungry customers dissatisfied. Even though he would have to clean up the kitchen again, Yab decided to serve them.

"Grab a seat. I'll be with you shortly."

"Are you sure?" the boy asked.

"We don't want to cause you any trouble," the girl pitched in.

"I'm sure," Yab said. "Miss out on the opportunity to feed you guys a good meal? Nah! Doesn't sound like me!"

Without further objection, the young couple took a seat. Yab cleaned their table and was ready to take their order.

The couple studied the menu, and the girl finally spoke. "Do you have any plant-based dishes other than traditional salads?" the girl asked. "Alex doesn't eat meat."

"It's okay," the guy said. "I'll just take a salad."

"I'm afraid we don't," Yab said. "However, I could cook you a plant-based chicken burger if you want. I do have the necessary ingredients."

The couple exchanged a surprised look.

"I thought you didn't have any plant-based dishes," Alex said.

"Well…we don't. It's not on the menu, but it would be a pleasure to cook you something worthy of your time," Yab said.

"Thank you, sir," Alex said.

"I'll take one as well," the girl said, handing him the menus.

"Right away." Yab returned to the kitchen and grabbed the ingredients from the fridge.

Every time he cooked, Yab became one with the kitchen, his mind escaping reality into a world of happiness, serenity, and bliss. Despite his irregular and sparse sleep, when it came to cooking, Yab forgot about everything, his mind blazing, alight with passion.

He forgot about the hardships of his daily life and only focused on making the best vegan chicken burgers he could, letting his passion show through his work. He envisioned the couple tasting the burgers and thanking him for the meal, the image vivid in his mind.

Once the burgers were ready, Yab served them to the couple. They both turned with a similar expression to Victor's when he first laid eyes on the burger. Then, with ravenous appetites, they dove right in, each taking a big bite.

After a very short pause, the girl broke the silence. "This is probably the best vegan burger I've ever had," she said.

"I am a strict vegan, and I have eaten many plant-based burgers. This is one of the best I have ever had." Alex said with enthusiasm. "You should add it to the menu!"

The girl silently nodded in agreement.

"I'll ask Mr. Victor. If he agrees, we'll definitely do it."

"What's the secret?" the girl asked.

"It's in the spices and chilies I use to marinate it," Yab explained. "Along with the texture and, of course, my secret sauce you see on top. That's half the flavor."

"See, I told you," the girl said to the boy. "The sauce is delicious!"

"Hope you enjoyed your meal," Yab said, piling their empty plates.

"Oh, we did," Alex said with a content smile.

"We will definitely be back for more," the girl added.

After the couple left, Yab returned to the kitchen, humming and singing, cleaning the remaining pots, pans, and plates with newfound enthusiasm and joy. He didn't know where this sudden surge of exhilaration came from. A few hours ago, all he wanted to do was go home and sleep. Now, he felt alive, eager to cook again. Maybe it was the excitement about the plant-based dishes or the joy of sharing a good meal. He couldn't quite put his finger on it.

While the source of the blissful feelings alluded Yab, he hoped that they would linger a little longer, fueling his time in the US with inspiration and confidence.

Yab decided he would make the best of his time there and returned home with the brightest smile he'd worn since coming to America.

Yab thought about the ceiba tree and his family's creed... He thought about how his father's explanation that the branches represented having expertise at something, and while giving the spinner a whirl, he came up with this new affirmation:

"I am on an accelerated track to success, as I am an expert at plant-based food."

9

THE WARRIOR AWAKENS

Yab woke up to the sound of the phone, ringing in the distance. He sat up with difficulty, his mind still out, begging to get back to sleep. He yawned and stretched before fully realizing what time it was.

Very few had his number, and no one would call in the middle of the night. Was it Victor? Did something happen in the restaurant?

Yab lurched up and grabbed the phone hastily.

"Hello?" Yab asked with a hoarse voice. "Mr. Victor?"

"Yab…" It wasn't Victor's voice. It was his mother, her voice deeply troubled.

"Mama, is everything all right?" Yab asked, a fearful rush running through him.

There was a long, agonizing pause that served as a portent of grave news.

"Mom, what is it?" Fear came alive in Yab's voice, and his face changed completely.

"Your dad," his mother said and paused again.

Yab closed his eyes shut, rubbing them, bracing himself for what was to come. He didn't want to hear what his mother had to say. The urge to flee took hold of him.

"Your dad is in the hospital," his mother said with a sob, shattering the silence.

"Is he all right? What happened?" Yab asked.

"We went to the doctor because his chest was hurting," his mother said. "Seems he had a heart attack recently. Yab, your dad's not doing well."

Yab held his breath and clenched the phone.

"What do the doctors say? Will he be all right?"

"They kept him for a week," his mother said. "They're not sure. They told me to mentally prepare for the worst. Everything is a possibility is what they said."

"Are you all alone? Is there anyone to help you?" Yab stood up, pacing inside his room.

"Your uncle is here. He decided to help since you're gone. He promised to take care of the house while we're in the hospital," his mother said.

Those words resounded on the back of his mind and hit his heart like a bass drum. *Since you're gone,* Yab thought, his jaw trembling with guilt. Yab remained silent, the onus of his choice resting heavily upon him.

"Yab, I have to go," his mother said. "The doctors called me in again."

"Let me know if anything changes," Yab said.

"I love you, Yab. Promise me that you'll take care of yourself."

"I will," Yab said. "I love you too, Mama."

The line went dead.

Yab was unable to sit back down. He kept pacing the room, thinking about his father.

I should have been there, Yab thought. What was Yab supposed to do? A desperate tear carved his cheek. If he left back home now, he might never have another shot at success. Coming to the US was a dire challenge–one he would have to repeat twice in order to return home and back to the US again. Yab wasn't pessimistic, but the idea itself seemed impossible. God and the spinner were by his side on his way here, and he made it, but he also knew that it wasn't wise to put them to the test. Deep in his heart, he knew that for good things to happen, he also had to play his part and not take foolish decisions.

It would take months to return to Copán. His father might already be dead and without the help he needed. Yab would sacrifice everything if he were to leave now, and he would be of no help back home. What could he do?

Yab sat on the edge of the bed and looked around the frugal, smelly room. *This wasn't my dream,* Yab thought, *living in a small apartment, with no heat, no proper plumbing, spending my precious time at a dead-end job.*

Yab came here to find a new industry, a new product as powerful and massive as coffee. But after all that time, he was no closer to that dream. Was this what he abandoned his family for?

Yab took the spinner from the nightstand into his hand and gave it a spin, watching the colors change and integrate into one: the warrior.

"What should I do?" he asked, watching the spinner turn with tears in his eyes.

Either he would be tough and persevere, face the challenge before him resiliently, or he would have to abandon his dream, return home, and lose his chance at success.

What could I even do if I headed back home? I'm not a doctor. I couldn't help him, Yab thought.

It was as if Abuelo's wisdom spoke through the spinner. All the aspects of the spinner worked together and soon enough, an answer presented itself in Yab's mind. An idea surfaced from the depths of his creative mind. The warrior brought him the answer–and a resourceful one at that.

Even if he returned home, he had no way of helping his family. His family needed him here, in the US. He would work harder, better, and smarter. He could save some extra money and send it to his family to pay for his father's needs. That would be a much bigger help. Yab would stall his dream but only momentarily. Once his father's health recovered, he would resume the pursuit of his dream; he wouldn't back down from the challeng–not now.

With the promise of sleep drifting away, Yab stood up, grabbed his coat, and stepped out in the middle of the cold night, heading for the neighborhood's Internet cafe. He would find another job, along with Victor's restaurant. He might not physically be there by his father's side, but he would support him in any way he could from afar, much like his father did all those years for him.

That was the least he could do for the people that raised him and supported him throughout his life, making him the man he was.

"Please, God, keep my father safe," Yab said, holding the spinner tightly in his hand.

He would help them at any cost.

10

RE-GOALED & RE-ENERGIZED

The sky had brewed a vehement storm of lightning and thunder. The first raindrops crashed against the window, the glass rattling with each forceful bead.

Yab stood up from the small office desk that came with the house and pushed the iron bucket, placing it under the caved part of the ceiling as he always did in days of rain. If not for the bucket, the rain pouring from the ceiling would form puddles on the ground and he would have to mop for hours on end.

Staring out the window, a frown carved its way through Yab's face. He used to love the rain–its scent and smell. The forests of Copán thrived on it, and the trees were dancing in the stormy winds. The entire forest radiated a smell of freshness, and the gloomy skies served as the best backdrop above the ruins.

Now, cold rain came with a musty, humid smell and a ruined wall full of black, watery marks: a painful reminder of his challenging life in the US.

With the bucket in place, Yab sat behind the old desk, pen in hand, ready to go through his expenses. The rent was due, and heat was a luxury at this point. He could skip heat for another month; he was never in the house anyway. Calculating his expenses, Yab realized he had to send a little more money to his family. His father's condition had improved, but the medical expenses were still high.

Yab sighed, leaning back, rubbing his bloodshot eyes. The same thoughts of conceding returned, as they did every time Yab felt swamped in expenses, imprisoned within the walls of his new life. Everything would be so simple if he just gave up. He could go back to Copán, enjoy his days in peace, without striving for much. He could have a good life.

Yab shook the thoughts away. That wasn't right. Abandoning his dream for comfort didn't feel right. He had to persevere. He had to stay positive. Yab looked at the spinner on the desk. As he did every time he felt his confidence waning, Yab grabbed it in his hand and caressed the sun's texture.

"I have to protect my inner dialogue," Yab said. "I will not be a victim of these dire circumstances. People who work hard get rewarded in the end; that's the truth!"

His smile returned. He had to push through. He had to fight. Leaving the sheet of expenses aside, Yab took his coat and prepared for his second job.

It was a rainy Saturday morning, and Yab had already reached the local university he had been working for as a janitor for the past six months. They were the only ones hiring through an under-the-table deal, and Yab took it without a second thought. He needed the extra income.

His free time went from scarce to non-existent. During the early hours, he cleaned the halls, classrooms, and labs of the university, and during the afternoon and until after hours he worked at Victor's restaurant.

His time at the shelter came to an abrupt end, as he could no longer fit two jobs and volunteering in his schedule. He worked to make a living and worked even more to provide for his family back home. And yet, Yab never forgot about the kids. Once his father's condition improved, Yab would provide some of the extra money to the shelter.

Many would have despaired already. Not Yab. He tried to make the most of the challenges. It was his newfound passion that kept him going. It was ironic how Yab had to move to the US to find his true love for the plant-based cuisine. If not for the new goal, Yab would have given up, probably. He was onto something, and he was willing to pursue it to the world's end.

One day at the University where Yab had to clean everything, from classrooms to the teacher's offices, and the hallways, he realized he had finished in half the time because there had been little to no activity the day before; which meant that, for once, he didn't have to leave in such a hurry for Victor's restaurant, so he decided to take it easy on his way out of the University, to catch his breath and relax a little. Yab returned his equipment to the janitor's closet and strolled down the pristinely clean hallways. Yab played with the spinner, watching the colors and how they blended into one solid whole. He gave it a spin and for some reason, his gaze left the spinner and looked at an open door on his right as if something was calling him from behind the door. It was a lab with industrial food equipment. As was natural for a Saturday morning, the lab was empty.

Yab's eyes moved from the spinner to the lab and back, and the warrior spoke to him. The warrior appeared, coated in the light of a brand-new idea, and handed Yab a course for an already existing goal, a resourceful path to follow up on a new recipe. Yab suddenly felt the energy to make the most of his recent challenge, and Yab wouldn't let this opportunity slip through his fingertips.

He could get into trouble for entering the lab, so he thought and weighed his options. He wouldn't destroy any of the equipment, Yab presented a counter-argument. He would only take a look.

Yab entered the modern lab, inspecting the available equipment. It featured everything a top-tier food manufacturer company would for research and development. Yab had toyed with the idea of buying some of these machines for his restaurant back in Copán, but it was an unnecessary expense at the time, as they would have rarely been used. Like a child on the playground, Yab inspected the equipment, imagining what he could do with each one, his smile growing. Among the burnished machines, one caught Yab's attention, and he made his way over like a moth to the flame.

It was a rotary drum, sitting at the far end of the lab, and Yab's jaw dropped at the realization. He heard about food scientists using rotary drums to create vegetable protein flavoring without changing the texture, and he knew how a chef like himself could produce wonders with it, especially to make the base of his secret sauce.

The idea of getting into trouble vanished in an instant. Even if he were caught fiddling with the machine, he could explain his intentions. A stream of ideas surged through Yab's brain, making it impossible to think of any of the ramifications if he got caught. He had to put his idea to the test.

Hastily, Yab bolted out the door, heading to the nearest grocery store to gather the ingredients he would need for his first experiment.

Yab returned with a bag full of organic flours, and after making sure that no one was around, he closed the door and spread the contents all over the counter. With a couple of extra hours between his janitorial shift and the start of his shift at Victor's, Yab was ready to begin the first test.

One of the greatest challenges of the plant-based kitchen was substituting the dairy options. Seemingly, nothing could substitute the cheesy flavor many dishes featured, but with the rotary drum at his disposal, Yab knew that he could use yeast to emulate this flavor without using any dairy products.

Yab put the machine to work and added the yeast and all the other food inside the rotary drum, setting it to work, while he turned his attention to his sauce. He had never had access to a rotary drum, and Yab always felt that his sauce could use a hint of cheese flavor. The yeast would serve that purpose, acting as a binding agent at the same time, taking the place of butter.

Separately, Yab prepared the remaining ingredients and set a pot to boil. When the rotary drum's work was over, Yab added the fresh blend inside the sauce. The flavors evaporated into Yab's nose, mixing with the spices. The yeast worked, thickening the sauce, and turning it into a more burger-appropriate condiment.

In less than an hour, Yab had the new sauce steaming-ready in the pot. He took a spoonful. His entire face cringed at the new taste. While the yeast worked, it produced a smoked result, a very unexpected one. He could use this sauce in a salad, but not in his burger. Despite its improvable taste, it still tasted like progress.

He didn't expect the new recipe to be a success from the first try, and Yab was now more determined than ever to succeed. He found a new goal to work toward, and he just figured out some of the tools to achieve that. He would work, and he would work hard until he had a perfect result in his hands–the healthiest solution possible.

Yab was happy for the epiphany and having access not only to the tools to use toward his success but also obtaining greater clarity of the potential before him.

With a new breath of energy, after cleaning everything up, Yab headed straight to Victor's restaurant.

• • •

Despite the trials of his daily life, Yab felt alive every time he stepped into Victor's kitchen. The past few months, the two grew close as work partners and friends, and Victor entrusted Yab with everything kitchen-related.

Yab was the first to open the restaurant, and he took the time to prepare the kitchen with diligence. He chopped the vegetables; prepared the marinades, the beans, and the chili peppers; and placed the pots and pans on the ovens. He felt at home whenever he had to cook and prepare meals for the customers.

After Alex and his girlfriend came to the restaurant a few more times, bringing a few of their friends along, always praising Yab's delicious burger, Victor was willing to add a few of the plant-based dishes to the menu. It took some time, but the plant dishes progressively attracted more interest.

With his plant-based dishes slowly becoming a hit, more people swarmed to taste the plant-based burger and other vegan concoctions. A good country steak was available everywhere, but a good plant-based dish was hard to find; especially one made by the hands of a Mayan cook with all his tricks and particularities.

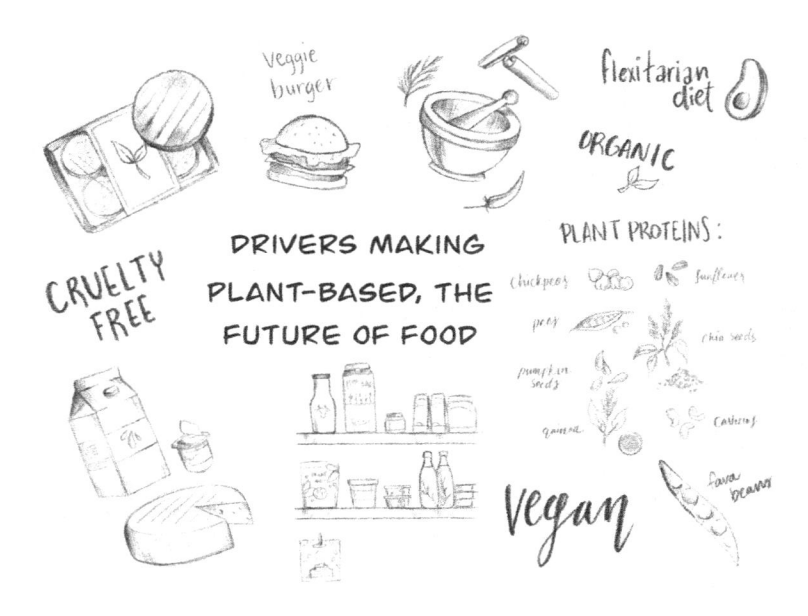

Looking back, Yab would have never thought that there was so much demand for something he found so ordinary–mundane even– from his native land. Back home, they used the plant-based alternative because of the low price and health benefits to the poorest of clients. Many chefs had adopted this approach, Yab among them; but it never felt like an untapped market–only another approach that surged out of necessity.

• • •

With such a high demand for plant-based dishes in the US, Yab found himself cooking, training, and practicing the plant-based arts–because it was a form of art of his *own*.

His knowledge was still rudimentary, but he always found a spark of inspiration in the kitchen to experiment and tackle culinary problems from various angles. Some experiments worked, others not so much, but at the end of the day, the customers left with a satisfied smile that warmed Yab's heart, reminding him of why he chose to be a chef.

Yab always made sure to let his fire and passion show through his best work. His work was a small reminder of his calling, and that's why he loved working at the restaurant, exploring something new–an unexplored field where his creativity and passion could shine.

For almost two years, Yab worked tirelessly and invested his best efforts and time into his new passion. There wasn't a single moment throughout the day that Yab wasn't thinking about the plant-based cuisine.

Every Saturday, Yab powered through his janitor shift in order to get those extra couple of hours in the University's Lab, experimenting on his sauce. By this point, the Chemistry professors had already discovered Yab and his shenanigans, but after one of them approached Yab, they all became so thrilled about his story, that they decided to look the other way if they ever saw him in the lab–plus, he always left everything in perfect order and proved to be shrewd when managing the material. With every mistake came more knowledge, and Yab was growing more proficient at using the equipment.

On his second birthday in the US, Victor gifted him a book of plant-based recipes.

"This is a gift, a sign of appreciation, and an investment," Victor said. "I never thought these vegan dishes you young people eat would sell so well, but I was wrong."

Yab looked at the book and smiled with tears in his eyes. "Thank you so much, Mr. Victor."

"You care about this restaurant as much as I do. It's the least I could do," Victor patted him on the shoulder. "Keep doing what you do best, kid."

Yab didn't have enough time to study the book at home, but he always consulted it while in the restaurant. Sometimes he was even eager to head to work and flip through the brand-new pages of the book, learn a new recipe, and try a new combination.

One night that was a little slower than the rest, with just a few customers in the restaurant, Yab had enough time to follow one of the recipes found in the book for plant-based chicken. The result was astounding. He tasted it and offered a free plate–as per Victor's instructions–to all the customers. The feedback was overwhelmingly positive.

Yab was ecstatic. No matter how much he loved to improve his plates through trial and error, the book proved to be an invaluable guide to further improve his craft. That's when Yab realized that he was no longer satisfied with his progress so far. He could do so much more than a simple plant-based chicken. He wanted to perfect his sauce and the techniques required for plant-based cuisine. There was a single way to overcome this frustration and promote his personal growth.

Breathless and with his heart pounding, Yab skipped out of the kitchen straight into Victor's office.

"Yab, my friend," Victor said, lowering his newspaper. "Are you all right? You seem a little excited. What happened?"

"Mr. Victor," Yab spoke sharply. "I have a favor to ask."

"Shoot," Victor said.

"The restaurant has been going quite well recently," Yab said.

"I'm not sure if I can give you a raise just yet," Victor said, raising his hand and stopping him abruptly.

"That's not what I'm here for," Yab said. "I want to study in a culinary school!"

"You want to study?" Victor asked, raising an eyebrow in disbelief. "What's wrong with what you already know?"

"I can't afford to study, but I can't stop thinking about it," Yab said, with his mind on fire. "I want to enroll and study about all the vegan recipes and help you out, making the restaurant even better!"

Victor smiled. "I'll tell you what," Victor said. "You have poured your heart and soul into my restaurant, treating it as your own. Not to mention that we're no longer in debt. I never thought the restaurant could be a sheer success. We still don't offer the steak I like, but I'm willing to let this one slide since you do such amazing work here," Victor said with a chuckle. "I'm happy to call you my friend, so I want to help you out. I can let you work a few extra shifts here and there to earn some extra money for your school, but you have to promise not to start cooking for a competitor and not to forget about your job here when you catch others' interest!."

Victor and Yab shared a laugh. "Of course, no competitors–I promise."

Yab was thrilled. He couldn't hide the excitement beaming across his face.

"But I'll do you one better," Victor said. "Because culinary schools here are very expensive, I can vouch for you, so you can get a small private loan. What do you say? We'll pay it together in due time."

Yab didn't have to think about it.

"Thank you, Mr. Victor," Yab leaned almost with reverence, grabbing his hand in a tight handshake.

"No need to thank me. If only everyone was as eager as you to learn and provide…" Victor said. "Now, go back to the kitchen because the customers are hungry. Let me know if you find a school, okay?"

"You won't regret this," Yab said and almost skipped back to the kitchen.

Yab went home that night and wrote almost a dozen cover letters for every culinary school in the area. With Victor's recommendation letter to accompany his applications, Yab was certain that his future would shift. He would escape the predicament of US life and dictate his own future, on his own terms.

Yab held the spinner in his hand and thanked Abuelo for the valuable lessons he taught him, thinking about the Inner Warrior and the bright ideas that came to mind. Yab recited the following Mantra until he fell asleep with a bright smile on his face.

"I will give myself an edge by going back to school and learning new techniques that will help me achieve my goals."

11

YAB'S MOUNT OLYMPUS

Like almost every day, Yab woke up before the first crack of dawn to prepare for his janitor's shift. He emptied the bucket of stagnant rainwater, cleaned off the restaurant's scent with a cold bath, and put on the janitor's uniform.

Heading out the front door, Yab noticed an envelope among the bills. Noticing the name of one of the culinary schools he'd applied for. Yab held his breath, barely able to crouch and grab the letter. He had to muster all his courage to do so.

With a quick breath, Yab grabbed the envelope, tore it open, and eagerly grabbed the letter within. His eyes skimmed through the introduction, and then his heart sank.

We are sorry to inform you that due to your immigration status, you are not allowed to enroll in our classes as per the state's rules and regulations.

That was the first response he got back in a week, but Yab didn't lose his faith. It was a small inconvenience. *At least one application will be accepted,* he thought. He stored the letter in the desk drawer and left for his shift.

The days went by, and the rejection letters kept piling up. Each rejection weighed heavier than the last, threatening to crush him with despair. With each envelope he opened, with each "We are sorry to inform you" that he read, his chances of growing as a cook and improving his craft looked farther away.

• • •

Six months. Six long months of rejections. Yab was sitting on the couch with the pile of crumpled-up rejection letters before him. His mind was finally blank, and he felt utterly defeated. There was not much he could do anymore. All he wanted was to close his eyes and rest…to forget about his problems, his goals, his aspirations–to simply forget about everything.

Yab wanted to recite his mantra one more time, but the words had lost their meaning, feeling stale and old.

What if his Abuelo had been wrong? What if it wasn't so simple? Yab sighed. He didn't want to think like that about his Abuelo, but life hadn't left much of an option. As he slowly closed his eyes, surrendering to the battering exhaustion, a soft knock came on the door.

Yab opened his eyes slowly, thinking that the knock had been a knock, but another knock came. Yab dragged his feet to the door only to find a mailman standing outside, shifting through his leather bag.

"Are you Mr. Pineda?" the mailman asked.

Yab nodded.

The mailman handed him a letter, bid him farewell, and started down the staircase.

Yab looked at the letter. It was from another culinary school he had applied to. *Another rejection,* Yab thought. Yab didn't even feel anxious this time. He knew what the letter would have to say. He simply opened the letter and skimmed through the introduction, ready for the inevitable rejection.

But...what was this? Yab read the last paragraph again, unable to believe what he had seen. It *wasn't* a rejection.

Mr. Pineda, it is with great pleasure that we inform you that our culinary school would be pleased to have you. Due to your immigration status, we are not allowed to officially enroll you in any of our classes, but we want to make an exception and provide you with a special permission of attendance for the rest of the year. If your immigration situation is resolved by the time of enrollment next year, we would be glad to officially enroll you in our classes with all the student privileges and perks so you can further your education and attend all classes offered in our school.

Yours truly,

Dean of Admissions.

Yab couldn't contain the cheer building up inside him. He raised his hands to the sky, crying with joy. His hands and legs were shaking, and he could barely breathe. He made it! He'd been accepted into culinary school!

Yab lurched on the phone and first called Victor, and then his Abuelo, and shortly after, he informed his mother and father. They were all proud of his accomplishment–probably even more so than Yab was of himself.

Once the original sensation of joy and relief had settled, Yab felt ashamed for having lost faith in Abuelo's words. Even in the darkest of times, Abuelo's wisdom proved superior.

Without losing any time, Yab started preparing for his first day of culinary school.

12

ANOTHER TEST

For three long years, he had fought, working hard–harder than ever before in his life. With total faith in God, his mantra, and his own strength, Yab achieved things he had never deemed possible.

His life had finally been set straight. Despite juggling two jobs and culinary school, Yab had never felt more alive in his entire life.

Every day, he woke up at 8 a.m., took the bus to the culinary school, and attended his classes, actively participating and experimenting in the kitchens with all kinds of ingredients and flavors, learning from the young, larger-than-life students, and asking all the questions he had amassed over the years. Out of sheer passion and hard work, Yab was one of the brightest students there, hence the school quickly became interested in Yab and wanted him to officially enroll in their program; naturally, they wanted bragging rights associated with such a young talent. Under the current conditions, however, that didn't appear to be possible.

As one of his teachers said, "The school is lucky to have you. Once you make a name for yourself, the school will be privileged to boast that you were a student here!"

Yab still wasn't an official student. He had a grace period in which he could attend all classes and work alongside his other classmates, but soon enough, he would have to resolve his immigration status if he wanted to further pursue his studies. But at that moment, Yab wasn't thinking about that. He was only thinking how deeply blessed he was to have access to such privileged education.

Despite spending most of his time in a busy, quick-paced lifestyle, Yab never forgot the reason he enrolled in the first place. He wanted to improve his skills as a chef, most importantly, to further refine his recipes to better serve his customers.

Amongst the many exams, classes, and study sessions, Yab always found some time to speak to his teachers about the recipes he was working on. One of the instructors, Miss Julianna, was fascinated enough with Yab's attempts to create his own sauces for his traditional and vegan chicken system.

"We rarely get students as curious as you," Miss Julianna said. "It's always refreshing to see that some chefs still care about every product they put on a plate!"

Between classes and on slow days at school, Yab would sit down with Miss Julianna, explaining a recipe he had learned empirically through painstaking trial and error. Miss Julianna, a skilled chemist among other things, was kind enough to correct the smoky taste that continued to plague Yab's sauce.

"We'll also try to marinate the meat first, an additional step being used by the big boys out there! "You see, Yab, it's a set of elements that make the overall taste of the dish not only one ingredient."Are you familiar with kimchi as an element to marinades?"

"No, I have never heard of it," Yab said.

"This is a little advanced, but you're far above your grade already, "Miss Julianna said.

Miss Julianna explained the benefits of kimchi, both in the culinary world and in the health aspect. She explained everything about the fermentation process and how it could be used as a step prior as a marinade and would take more preparation time. A skilled cook like Yab should be able to use Kimchi adequately after only a few tries.

With Julianna's many years of experience in the field and Yab's innate expertise regarding flavor and taste, Yab managed to perfect his chicken system and sauce over the course of his first year in the culinary school, working tirelessly with various experiments and tests, all approved and guided by his encouraging teacher.

After they were both satisfied with the results of the system as a whole, Yab attempted to use it in Victor's restaurant. None of the clients were informed of any changes–not even Mr. Victor. And as expected, the recipe's new secret ingredient seemed to be an overwhelming success with the customers.

Victor entered the kitchen hastily, looking around, smelling the boiling pots with a puzzled expression.

"What, did you change to the recipe?" Victor asked.

Yab only smiled at him. "A few customers keep telling me how they love the new chicken burger," Victor said. "Did we change the burger?"

"I might have altered the process a bit," Yab said.

"Altered?" Victor said. "Why? The previous one was great!"

Yab pointed at one of the pots.

"Taste it for yourself," Yab said.

Victor took a spoon and tasted the new marinade. The spoon fell out of his hand and he turned with disbelief in his eyes.

"Is this even possible…I thought the food couldn't get any better!" Victor said.

Yab bowed with appreciation.

"Use it on every dish you can!" Victor said. "I tell you, this will be our goose of the golden eggs !"

Yab laughed, "It's not that good yet, but I'll experiment with it."

"It's better than you think it is," Victor said, slowly leaving the kitchen, murmuring in utter amusement.

And so they did. Yab started using the new sauce, along with the new techniques and dishes he had learned in culinary school, and the reward was immediate. More customers surged to the store, and it gradually became a trending destination.

Victor was more than satisfied, giving Yab some extra money here and there when the situation allowed it. The customers were uniformly satisfied, always returning for Yab's delicious plant-based dishes, which only continued to improve in quality and technique, prompting many customers to commend the new and improved sauce. From an underground restaurant, Victor's restaurant became a must-go destination in the area.

During the entire year as a student, Yab experienced stability. His work at Victor's restaurant armed him with experience, the culinary classes expanded his knowledge and understanding of plant-based cuisine, and his time in the lab fed his creative curiosity. Finally, Yab was actively working toward his goals, and soon enough, once he had polished all the tools at his disposal, Yab would be able to tackle the bigger goals he had set, with no obstacles in his way. Success was waiting.

Yab could visualize it. He would become the best plant-based chef ever, and people would travel across the country to taste his dishes. With Victor by his side, they would be able to achieve anything that they set their minds to. Yab smiled at the idea.

***

"I let my fire and passion shine through my best work: to become the best chef in the world and provide the best food–vegan or not–to all my beloved customers."

Yab was determined to make the plant-based cuisine his specialty, and considering the fact that he came from a background of making the best chicken in town, he was driven by the idea of making his plant-based dishes, such as the nuggets and the vegan chicken sandwich, taste as good and savory as real chicken. This became central to his project. However, Yab never forgot his native cuisine, which he also cherished and loved preparing for his Latino customers.

It was just another Friday afternoon when Yab returned home, took a bath, and changed into his restaurant outfit. He was a few minutes late, but he was already about to head out the door when his cell phone rang.

"Yab, where are you?" Victor said from the other end of the line.

His voice was anxious, the words slipping slowly out of his mouth.

"Mr. Victor," Yab said, exhausted, barely moving his lips. "I'm on my way. Sorry for being late."

"That's not why I called you," Victor said, his voice defeated. "I have some bad news."

Yab felt his knees shaking. What could have happened?

"ICE came in today," Victor said.

Yab felt the blood freezing in his veins, a cold shiver running through his body.

"They found out that you've been working here illegally," Victor said. "They threatened me with fines and charges."

Victor's voice cracked, "If you work another day here, they... they'll deport you and shut the place down...I'm so sorry," Victor said.

"H-how did they find out?" Yab asked, more thinking out loud than posing an actual question.

"I have no idea," Victor said.

Victor kept talking, fast and anxiously, but Yab couldn't hear a word that was being said. It had to be the university. For three whole years, Yab led a normal life until he decided to enlist in the university. What was he thinking? It had been so long living in the US that he forgot that he was an undocumented immigrant just like most people crossing the border. He wasn't any better than them.

That was a blow that shattered everything. Tears streamed from his eyes. His internal dialogue was now full of negativity, blaming himself, blaming his ambition, judging his choices. Yab dragged his feet and fell onto the couch.

"I'm truly sorry," Victor said. "But the restaurant is my only source of income."

"It's all right, Mr. Victor," Yab said with a defeated voice. "Thank you for sticking your neck out for me anyway."

Victor sighed in relief. It was hard for him as much as it was hard for Yab.

"Thank you for understanding," Victor said. "You were the damn best employee I've ever had. If there's anything I can do–"

"It's all right," Yab said. "It was an honor to meet you, Mr. Victor. I could try running away to another state, but what's the point? They'll find me sooner than later, and it will only cost me more money that I don't have. I'll never be a proper part of this land. Maybe I'll just head home this time."

Yab hung up the phone, sobbing. When everything was about to take a good turn, life didn't want to reward him for his struggles and sacrifices. Yab held the spinner and gave it a turn. He asked the Mayan sun to keep his mind clear of all the negative thoughts. His goals were still there. It was just a small bump in the road–a minor setback. Nothing he couldn't overcome. Somehow he had to find a way to persist.

Maybe he would go home, spend time with his father, his cousins, and the rest of his family. Maybe family quality time was the point his father was trying to make before Yab left.

Yab remained positive. Even this setback could have silver linings. Nonetheless, he wasn't ready to leave everything behind, but eventually, he had to, and the sooner he wrapped his mind around the idea of leaving, the better. So he rotated the spinner, two, three times, letting all the colors become one, staring at it. There was one last thing he had to do before he left. That was the only way he would leave with a smile and on his own terms.

13

INTERNAL DIALOGUE STORM

With the same backpack he came to the US with strapped around his shoulders, Yab left his humble apartment, ready for another journey. This time, the trip would bring him back home, where he belonged. Before leaving, Yab decided to pay one last stop to the orphanage.

He couldn't remember when the last time was that he crossed its iron fence door leading into the untidy garden. Upon his arrival, the same familiar faces flashed their bright, inviting smiles, greeting him with enthusiasm. Beautiful memories and warm feelings overwhelmed his heart as he stared at the kids, who had grown tremendously and now looked ready to join the world.

Yab felt sorry for and inspired by them at the same time. They would have to leave the shelter and experience the dark side of the "American Dream," but their minds were still young and ambitious, eager to conquer the world.

Yab's heart stirred. The children had never left the orphanage, and some were doomed to spend their adolescence there, but they didn't despair. They tried to find joy in the simplest of things, and Yab's arrival lifted their spirits and dispelled their frowns. If his presence alone could make so many children happy, Yab thought that he might have achieved one of his goals after all.

Despite everything he had been through, the failures and sadness, Yab felt grateful to stand among the shelter's children. He might have forgotten why he strived all those months, but now he could see the answer clearly before him.

As the children dragged him inside, telling him stories, asking him to play games, and begging him to cook another burger for them, Yab cracked. Tears flowed down his cheeks. They weren't tears of sorrow but tears of joy. He remembered why he came here in the first place—why he fought. Abundance, not only for himself but also for all the people around him.

Yab gathered all the children and the shelter's volunteers around, wiping the tears from his eyes.

"I have some bad news," Yab said, and his voice cracked at the innocent, pure faces staring at him. "I have to go, for good. They're sending me back to Honduras."

Some children frowned, and others squirmed. The volunteers, having seen many immigrants coming and going, stared with eyes of compassion and genuine sadness.

"The truth is that I should have spent more time with you all, getting to know you better, seeing you grow and flourish. As much as

I hate to admit it, I fell victim to the circumstances and the stable life I managed to achieve. Many distractions appeared in my way, good and bad. Ultimately, I lost track of my original purpose. It wasn't my own success that I wanted to pursue but the success of anyone less fortunate than me, and for forgetting that, I am truly sorry," Yab said, smiling bitterly. "You all taught me more than you can imagine–about myself and about the way I see the world now. Beauty can lie in the least expected places, and you all taught me what true beauty is."

Then, they relished memories of the past, sharing stories, playing games once again as if nothing had changed since the last time he was there.

"But before I go," Yab said, standing before the small crowd. "Would you let me cook one last meal for you guys?"

The children and volunteers cheered. They helped set the tables and chairs and pulled the portable kitchen into the center of the shelter. Yab took out his spices, chili peppers, his finally-perfected sauce, and two green grocery bags, and placed them on the table. Surrounded by young kids eager to help, Yab gave them instructions and started to work.

They cooked till sundown, and when night fell, they feasted like Mayan kings. Yab poured his heart and soul into his final meal in the US, and it proved the finest feast he ever prepared: plant-based burgers and vegetarian chicken nuggets, paired with fresh salads and his secret sauce, sweet potato fries, and even a few of his plant-based chicken filets. All the knowledge and experience Yab had accumulated during his stay in the US was on the table.

Yab stared at the beaming, insatiable children, eating, laughing, and asking for more.

"I let my fire and sun show through my best work," Yab murmured to himself with a bittersweet smile. *"I will develop abundance for many whether I'm in the US or back home…"*

In the sweet, sweaty throes of exhaustion, Yab sat outside the shelter, staring at the night sky, looking at the faint stars. *The stars aren't as bright here*, he thought. That was the same with his goals. They hadn't been as bright for a while, but he was starting to see them more clearly once again.

In the shelter's yard, Yab noticed a man that didn't seem to belong there. He was wearing a fine suit and tie, along with cufflinks, shiny shoes, and a confident smile. Two of the shelter's volunteers approached him and after a quick discussion, they pointed toward Yab.

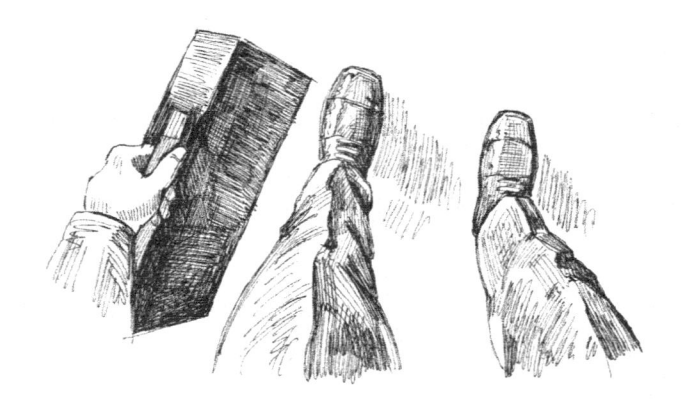

The man approached, chest puffed and shoulders spread, walking like a company executive. Finally, he stopped before Yab. "You're Mr. Pineda, I assume?" the man asked.

Yab nodded apprehensively, "You're here to take me away, aren't you?"

The man burst into loud laughter.

"No, no, I'm here to help!" the man said with a reassuring smile.

Yab raised an eyebrow of suspicion. Back home, these types of people were not to be trusted, and they usually proved bearers of bad news.

"Excuse my ill manners," said the man, extending his sizable hand. "My name's Phil Duncan."

Yab shook away, still trying to figure out the mysterious man's motives.

"Sorry if I startled you," Phil continued. "I stopped by the restaurant, but Mr. Victor told me you no longer work there. He gave me your address and said that this was the only other place where I might find you."

"Who are you?" Yab asked. "And why were you looking for me?"

Phil smiled and asked with a simple gesture if he could sit beside Yab. Yab nodded and made some space on the wooden bench for the man to sit.

"I'm an impact venture capital investor," Phil said

"A what?" Yab asked.

"I find promising, early-stage concepts, coach the entrepreneurs, and invest in their ideas. I make sure that startups make an exponential impact in the world," Phil said. Picking up on Yab's nervousness, he hastened to further explain. "Don't worry. You'll quickly understand who I am and that I'm only here to share some good news."

"I don't have a start-up," Yab said. "I'd *like* to have one, but I don't. I think you might be looking for someone else."

"I think you do have one in mind, but you simply haven't had access to the right tools to make it happen. Not yet, at least," Phil reassured him.

Yab eyed him closely. This man seemed to know an awful lot about Yab's goals.

"I was once poor. I certainly don't come from the richest of backgrounds," Phil said with a gentle look on his face. "Some people have wonderful ideas, but no one really invests in them; no one dares to give them a chance. I know it's not easy in this world, is it? Not everyone gets a fair chance at life."

"No, no it's not," Yab said, still apprehensive.

"I came from nothing, and I was lucky to meet some great people along the way. Benefactors, mentors–opportunity really shined on me.

"So, Yab, I learned that you were forced to leave Victor's Restaurant; and the volunteer that brought me to you also told me that you're going back home," Phil said. "But I also know you're an expert at preparing plant-based foods. Which explains the reason for my visit today: Did you know that plant-based food production is becoming a billion-dollar industry? That's why I want to invest in you and your talent. I've been meaning to reach out for a while now, but I had to run it by my managers. So, I have a proposition for you; one I think you're going to like!"

"Why me? How did you learn about me?" Yab asked.

"I believe you're aware of a good customer of yours, Alex?" Phil asked with a smile.

"Oh, yes, I do remember him," Yab said. "Great kid."

"Alex happens to be my son, and he's also a big enthusiast of the plant-based cuisine, as are many people his age," Phil explained. "You see, my dear Alex, young and ambitious as he is–much like you–has shown me that there are so many things in the world we haven't explored yet. Millennials truly care about more things than we old-timers do. Plant-based cuisine is one of them, caring for the environment and the wellbeing of animals, etc. My son is really impressed by your recipes."

"So, that's how you found me?"

"Well, if it weren't for Victor notifying me about the recent ICE visit, I wouldn't have come rushing to find you. I wasn't sold on the idea at first," Phil said. "You see, I'm growing older, and as the years go by, I grow more hesitant of new things. But that's the beauty of youth: They think fearlessly. Alex brought some leftovers last time and once I tried the burger...you, my friend, had me fooled. I thought it was a chicken burger, and once Alex revealed it was a plant-based dish, I was stunned. I wouldn't have been able to tell the difference. That's when I realized how many things can be achieved through plant-based cuisine, and I started doing my research. There's an entire–still growing–market out there, and its customers are hungry for more alternatives; plus vegan diets have the lowest carbon footprint, a cause which I'm personally fond of!"

Yab smiled at the idea. Phil was right. Plant-based cuisine was an entire universe–and an expanding one at that. Yab was grateful enough he was a student of this cuisine, as he came from a region blessed with the richest soil to produce delicious spices, plants, and vegetables.

"So, I want to get to the point. From what I gathered, you plan to return to Central America?"

"I wouldn't say *plan* is the correct word; they didn't leave me much of a choice," Yab said, blowing some steam off. "Unfortunately, yes," Yab said.

"Immigration rules are a difficult maze for dreamers sometimes," Phil said with a somber nod, and then his smile dispelled the darkness. "But I want to help you get out of that maze."

"Help me how?"

"Our venture equity fund looks for promising industries that can impact the world. We recently decided to invest in plant-based foods, and your Mayan recipes could bring a great deal of innovative differential value to this market sector!

"Something else you'd be interested to know is that I'm personally invested in the challenges the US has with illegal immigration from your region, Yab, and I want to do something about it, as the rise in medical and social expenses will be unsustainable for the United States. Plus the human rights ramifications for your people are simply unbearable. There has to be a way to solve this issue in a mutually beneficial way–something that attacks the illegal migration issue at its root. We might, for instance, foster sustainable growth between the two regions and create economic opportunities between the US and Central America.

"And why exactly is a refined businessman such as yourself so concerned about the immigration issue?" Yab asked, skeptically.

My wife is from El Salvador, and I travel there all the time, and my heart melts for the land and its lovely people. The things I've learned that happen in those caravans…it's something I want to help stop. Also, it's motivating enough to try and keep families together in their home countries, through the creation of opportunity. I want to use our fund to help."

Yab was originally shocked at the man's willingness to help. He came out of nowhere and just offered to help in ways no one had so far in the US. Yab couldn't simply accept this fact. There had to be something more at play here. How could Yab simply believe that a benevolent and empathetic benefactor conveniently would appear in his life with perfect timing? Yab couldn't shake the feeling that there was some foul play involved–something bigger for Phil to gain. No seasoned businessman would be so eager to help.

Yab lowered his head, thinking about Phil's proposition. Scared, he shoved his hands into his pockets, and that's when his fingertip touched the spinner; the sun's texture was so smooth and calming. His Abuelo's words resounded in Yab's mind. It wasn't Yab talking but his subconscious, still wounded and hurt by his experience with Dominic. Yab had created a blind spot regarding benevolent entrepreneurs or potential business partners wanting to contribute. But should he listen to that blind spot? Should he trust it?

If Yab rejected Phil's proposition now, he would be back at square one, without enough money to pursue his dream, no way to stay in the US, nothing. But if Phil wanted to profit from his ideas, just like Dominic did, Yab would risk seeing his dream slip from his fingertips once again and another man making huge profits from his beloved child of an idea. Yab gripped the spinner tightly and asked God for a solution to his dilemma.

"So, what do you say?" Phil urged him.

Yab recalled the Mayan portrait Abuelo had in his living room, and he remembered he had to see beyond what met the eye.

The sun poured its light on Yab, dispelling the darkness around him. Yab could see clearly now. He could see the stars and the sky–his goals.

Even if Phil ended up stealing his ideas, at least his endeavors would be out in the world, serving millions of people, improving the lives of all, helping achieve abundance for all. That's what Yab wanted. It was his top priority. Even if it meant his idea belonged to someone else, Yab would sleep serenely every night, knowing that one way or another, he had succeeded in his cause, much like his Abuelo did with the macaws.

Nonetheless, even though he knew that his vulnerable position made him the underdog, Yab had learned from his past experiences and would try to protect himself at every turn, such as signing confidentiality contracts and not disclosing his ideas entirely and all at once but instead being strategic about them. "To tell you the truth," Yab said. "I came to the US with a dream. I wanted to make an impact in the world–find the new coffee industry to serve millions of customers".

"The new Coffee Industry?" Phil asked, puzzled. "What do you mean?"

"I wanted to discover a new product, something that was in such high demand that it would sell worldwide and create new opportunities for thousands of people…or for farmers back at home in my case. Coffee is a highly valued commodity worldwide, and it's our countries that produce the most delicious coffee seeds. Hence, this industry generates great opportunities for our region; I wanted to find something like this"

Yab paused and closed his eyes, envisioning his goal clearly in his mind. He looked up, and the stars were brighter now–as were his goals.

"However, I not only want to create a business; I also want to work with responsible trade. I don't want to leave the profits in the hands of just a few families who refuse to commit to decent prices for the farmers," Yab said, feeling once again the enthusiasm of his goal surging through. On another hand, there is a big portion of illegal immigrants that were unemployed farmers in Central America, so I believe that having access to a market as big as the US can help us build a positive correlation between market demand up here and rural areas' employment growth down there. I want to impact the world, one family at a time."

Phil listened with enthusiasm. He loved Yab's idea. Yab could tell. He smiled, already feeling the partnership flourish.

"How would you like to write a business plan for your idea and enter the impact investment venture challenge with me and my firm as sponsors?"

Yab laughed nervously. "I'm only a cook, I…I'm no entrepreneur. I don't know anything about business plans," Yab said, rubbing his neck with embarrassment.

"Worry not," Phil said with a new breath of exhilaration, standing up. "All you have to do is design the recipes, source the ingredients, and cook like you did for those people at the restaurant. We'll add the business aspects like tracking costs, determining prices at which we'll all make a profit, and strategizing how to scale the business. Yab, this is an opportunity not many get, and I want to help you. There is certainly a business interest on my part here, but I'd also cherish the opportunity to help you turn your situation around. Giving back is a natural reaction for me, dear to my heart, as a result of my background. I experienced a harsh upbringing, and I would've really appreciated a helping hand on my way up".

Yab held the spinner in his hand and thought about it. It all made sense now. He had the answer lying clearly before him. His past experiences worked with his goals and his passion, finally activating his creative mind to its fullest. Yab pictured the Copán fields, the food he used back in his restaurant, and the farmers.

"There is one thing I have to ask before we go any further with this idea."

"Now is your opportunity to speak; tell me," Phil said serenely.

"I don't want to use any old plant-based ingredients," Yab said.

"What do you mean?" Phil asked, almost confused.

"Not just *any* plant-based ingredients," Yab corrected. "I want to use *our* ingredients."

"I want to use our harvest from Central America–blessed with the best soil in the world; grown in great weather year-round; and tended by the purest, most noble, hardworking farmers I have ever met. We have a long tradition in agriculture, since the Mayan times. The Mayans, my ancestors, perfected mathematics to track eclipses and solstices, thus the change of seasons! The huge temples we see today were erected for this exact purpose. To earn the favor of the gods. In exchange, my ancestors sought to be blessed with adequate weather for farming their crops!"

Phil's eyes welled up at how Yab described his goal, with so much passion and reverence.

"I think it's time for the world to see all this accumulated knowledge, for many generations. I want this to be a global success," Yab said with a bright smile.

"This project can be a bridge," Yab said. *I can be that bridge.* We can help bring those amazing flavors to the world, starting with the US, where there are already so many Central Americans established, who will be glad to consume their national produce and which will naturally help us promote the initiative. The products I enjoyed while growing up…now everyone will be able to taste them and enjoy them as much as I did. The Plant-Based Revolution is the perfect opportunity to channel these Central American products, don't you think?"

Yab's smile had grown, ear to ear, and the two men exchanged a firm handshake of mutual respect and admiration.

"Yab, I think you're much more of a businessman than you admit," Phil said. "I'll come by tomorrow. Don't worry about ICE. As long as we work together, I'll arrange the legal details so that no one can give you any trouble."

Phil left the shelter's yard with a sincere look of admiration.

Yab smiled. He could finally see his dream taking shape before him, vivid as the macaws.

All it took was hard work, serving the people around him, never giving up, and gratitude. More than ever, he was sure he had found the new coffee industry. That night Yab came up with this affirmation:

"I have a positive expectation about my future partnerships and regard all previous negative experiences as learning opportunities. I am a great team player, and this allows me to achieve my goals of creating abundance for many."

14

IMPACT INVESTMENT VENTURE CHALLENGE

Phil secured an USCIS permit for Yab, giving him enough time and the right space to develop his idea in the US. For an entire year, Yab spent this time in the firm's incubator, working closely with Phil and his team to create the perfect business plan–a strategy capable of securing a victory in the impact investment venture challenge.

Since the early days of their collaboration, Phil explained the potential business plan they would follow, and they worked rigorously toward that. The first great milestone was preparing for the investment venture challenge, a competition for start-ups and seed-phase ideas. It was a small stepping stone–and Yab had learned a lot about taking small steps toward success–that even if it didn't go their way, it'd be useful–the exposure and feedback–to further improve the project. However, Phil reassured Yab that his team always won these competitions.

Yab had to learn a lot in a short period. His curious mind and his learning attitude represented an invaluable skillset, helping the entire team's effectiveness throughout the process. Having run his own restaurant, Yab definitely had business acumen, and Phil identified as much, happy to invest in his growth.

The year went by incredibly fast, and the day of the competition was soon closing in. Yab never doubted the knowledge he'd accumulated over the years. He felt ready to tackle bigger challenges now. And regardless of the result, on the inside, he'd learn and, therefore, succeed.

Yab found himself in the grand halls of the competition center: bright lights, cameras, and a cheering audience, young and old swarming to attend.

Phil couldn't accompany Yab at this point but made sure to go over the basic idea with him one last time before he took the stage.

Yab was now alone, sitting backstage, worried sick, but he didn't despair. He had faith in his idea, as much as Phil did. Yab wasn't so worried about the competition. He was worried because he finally had an idea that he truly cared about and that he wanted to manage perfectly. On top of that, this idea proved what his father had prophesied: that all that Yab had been looking for had always been back home. That was a wise piece of advice, and Yab could finally see it clearly. He prayed to God that his idea would get a fair chance; that's all he needed. A chance. That would be enough to walk toward his vision and take a step toward changing the world.

Many contestants came with wonderful ideas, but none was revolutionary enough to impact on a large scale. They came with fixes and solutions, but there was no real problem to begin with: coffee machine connected to the alarm clock, self-warming shoes, and a sock business gifting a pair of socks to the homeless for each pair someone bought from the company. *If someone could give the homeless a job and a place to stay, they wouldn't need the socks, to begin with,* Yab thought.

With the number of contestants thinning, Yab heard another round of applause drumming against his chest.

"Our next contestant comes from Copán," the announcer said. "Please, welcome to the stage...Mr. Yab Pineda!"

Yab took a deep breath, holding the spinner close in his pocket. He had everything he needed to succeed. He had prepared himself, he was passionate, he could see his purpose clearly forming before him. He was ready.

"I let my fire and sun show through my best work. I'll build a commercial bridge between the Mayan lands and the US, which will generate opportunities for the farmers and delight the consumers," Yab said, wearing his brightest smile and stepping onto the stage.

The lights blinded him, and the cameras forced a shiver down his spine. The people stood in silence, making Yab even more anxious.

"Welcome, Yab," the announcer said. "What is your sustainable business idea that will make an impact on the world? You may begin whenever you are ready."

Yab cleared his throat and began...

"Thank you, respectable judges and everyone present, for allowing me to be here. I want to present to you...Spice Society."

"Spice Society," the moderator echoed. "You've got the sexy name part nailed down–that's for sure! But what's it about?"

Yab gave a light chuckle and proceeded. "Our ultimate goal is to become a platform that eliminates systemic poverty in Latin America." With this, he stopped for a second to catch the judge's reaction to his larger-than-life statement. Their eyes were hooked on Yab, with looks that showed great anticipation.

Yab continued, confident about the bold statement as he cleared his throat. "We plan to achieve this by uniting small farmers and growers in Central America with consumers in the US by serving plant-based foods, spices, and chilis to vegan and vegetarian manufacturing companies."

"Plant-based foods represent a billion-dollar trend, growing and selling at a much quicker rate than any other traditional food product. This has consequently created a higher demand for spices and chili peppers because they add flavor to these vegan foods, such as plant-based burger patties and vegan nuggets, making them taste more like the original products.

"Food manufacturers, from startups to big multinationals, are innovating precipitously, inventing plant-based meats, eggs, and dairy products, among others. Currently, these manufacturers face various issues: On one hand, they have very limited sources of healthy, sustainable, and socially responsible plant-protein ingredients to work with, which are key qualities that these brands must integrate into their products in order to be consistent with their brand values. On the other hand, they have little knowledge of how plant-based flavors interact with each other according to their production processes.

"If you interview any plant-based food company, you will learn that their products haven't achieved their finest potential just yet. Despite that, plant-based products are being sold in bulk in almost every market. Most of the raw materials these manufacturers currently use are commodities that come far away from China and lack custom designs for each company's needs. That said, we have a better solution, which isn't just geographically closer than China–we're basically next-door neighbors."

"As far as the scope of the opportunity goes, in my culinary school, I learned that there are thirty million people in the US that have tried being vegetarian or vegan. This is an incredible amount, and it's on the rise: Any local supermarket's frozen aisle is proof of that, now having a plethora of plant-based options available.

"I am a flexitarian myself, and I bet that many in the audience here are too. We enjoy both vegan foods and animal products, and we mostly follow this diet for health and fitness reasons. What is truly shocking to me is that several studies have found that half of the US population is considered flexitarian. I am a chef, and my expertise is cooking plant-based foods. Most of my customers are between twenty-four and fifty years of age and love my recipes. The demand is simply unprecedented."

"Okay, okay! So, there's a market for it; we get it, but how will the Spice Society operate exactly?" the announcer asked.

"The Spice Society will sell specialty ingredients–business to business–serving the food brands and manufacturers that sell and cater their products to the vegan, vegetarian, and flexitarian consumers," Yab said. "For now, we've decided that we will not have a business-to-consumer direct brand. We'd rather focus on helping these manufacturers save research and development time and money, as our plant-based ingredients will already come with the perfect blend of plant protein, spices, and chili peppers and their determined flavors that we create in our own food lab.

"Another reason why we have established a link with Central American producers is that none of our crops can grow in the US due to weather; so they'll all be grown in the tropics, where we'll be able to produce them year-round.

"Central America might be known for suffering economic crises, but our soil is abundant and very rich! We can grow many types of plant proteins: chickpeas, chia seeds, peas, sunflowers, pumpkin seeds, quinoa, cashews, black beans and lupini beans, hemp seeds…and more are being studied while we speak!"

"The formulas used in our products will be custom-made by me and supervised by the best food engineers available.

"We will schedule annual visits to our plantations with our clients and seek to establish long-term relationships with them, but most importantly, we will create a sustainable community that will generate many jobs and opportunities in a region that is currently suffering from mass-emigration. We can create an impactful, sustainable, and scalable industry for a market that is skyrocketing and expected to reach $30 billion in a few years!"

"The way our sustainable community works is very simple. It begins with us recruiting small farmers that own 2-4 acres of land. We would provide them with seeds and top-notch planting techniques, along with generic and simple contracts, which would stipulate that they grow the crops on their land and sell to us at a fixed price.

"We'd bolster their entire agricultural process by providing technical assistance from our expert engineers in the field, aiming to make it sustainable.

"As daunting and bureaucratic as the processes might be, let's not forget about the incredible importance of executing a due diligence process through which we will verify organic certifications, clean water use, and water waste management.

"Ah! The most exciting part–the one which we all long for: the harvest phase! When the plants are ready to be harvested, we'll help the farmers with the logistics of getting the fresh crops to our stockpile plant, where we'll swiftly process the food and turn it into final products and fresh ingredients for the clients, all the while adhering to global regulations.

SPICES

HOT PEPPERS

PLANT-BASED PROTEIN

SAUCES

"By the way, when the factory is ready, I would love for you all to come visit it: the sights, the smell, and the friendly workers," Yab said passionately. "Together it all has the power to make anyone feel at home.

"Once the harvest is collected, farmers will receive their pay at the plant and can go home to rest for some time before they have to prepare for the next season, as we alternate crops.

"And what we finally get out of this long and collective effort is our final product portfolio, neat and ready for export to the US, and in many cases, it will be further processed stateside in our US factory to assure freshness and compliance with FDA requirements.

"Our clients will then receive our raw products delivered to their manufacturing plants in a timely manner, and those products will go into their production lines, and finally the consumer will be able to have the healthiest and best flavored plant-based foods in their favorite dishes.

"Now…I'll go ahead and address the huge question mark that's probably floating around in your heads: will we be profitable?

"Our revenue model is traditional and effective: growers charge us an amount in exchange for their harvest, and afterward we charge a higher fee to our food manufacturing customers, which covers all of our production overheads, assuring ourselves a solid profit margin.

"And as for logistics…I'm really not worried at all about them as there exist ample alternatives between Central America and the US. We're next-door neighbors, remember?

"I'm blessed to have met Phil, my partner, a seasoned impact investor with a fabulous team that have trained me over the past year so that I could stand in front of you today and present Spice Society. Phil's team is raising all the capital we need, drafting plans for infrastructure, and hiring a team of food scientists and sales experts to complement my certified culinary abilities. Phil will help me contact food manufacturer companies in the US, and we will visit them together in order to sign them as official clients.

"A very important first milestone we need to achieve is recruiting our first group of growers and farmers, and not only that, but we also want to do it in a geographically diversified manner among several Central American countries, so as to mitigate climate-change risks. These farmers are very humble and traditional people that are deeply rooted in their Mayan traditions and ancestral inheritance; therefore, we know it will take some convincing to get them on board.

"Additionally, they have never exported before and have experienced several disappointments while working for local companies that sought the richness of their traditional crops at the farmers' expense, which has caused an oversupply and plummeting prices. Such companies often fail to comply with the promised purchase price, leaving farmers to suffer huge losses. Oftentimes, this leaves them with no option but to deplete their emergency reserves, which can lead to disaster.

"However, we have devised a strategy that we think might work to counter these people's negative experiences, and it is based on the positive reputation my family has amongst the community. We'd basically try to transfer my families' core values unto the company and gain these farmers' trust, especially by avoiding making the same mistakes other companies have made with the coffee-growers of the region. I'd know because my dad is one of them. Coffee-growers are an iconic example of such a tragic process. They consider themselves victims of their countries' few corporate families, and therefore, they have slowly joined forces to create co-ops and buy expensive machinery, so they can export on their own. However, it has taken a century for them to progress this far, so we want to help our industry's farmers skip this unnecessary tedious process and find fair profit conditions and long-term sustainability for them and their families.

"As far as timing, the US has incredible educational and technical assistance programs already in place in Central America for small farmers.

"Central America has no other choice than to create job opportunities for our farmers. The entire region cannot immigrate to the United States. Heck, if it were up to me I wouldn't want one more soul to emigrate if it's going to be under such inhumane and dangerous conditions as the ones experienced in the infamous caravans. I was in one of them, and I dream of a day when no one has to go through what I did.

"Lastly, our *reason* for this beautiful project is the potential impact we can create in the community and perhaps even in the world, as this strategy is replicable. Besides providing growth, competitiveness, and employment in the communities we will work in, we will support environmental programs to secure the right use of water and energy in all of our processes.

"Additionally–and this is something dear to my heart–we will provide bilingual English education to our farmers' kids by building local schools and making sure that more Central American students are given the opportunity to excel, perhaps coming up with ideas and projects that will further help their communities. Likewise, I'm grateful for my parents who allowed me to learn English when I was a kid, I'm sure that this entire generation will also be grateful, as being bilingual can open unthinkable doors.

"I appreciate your patience with such a long plan, and now that I'm running out of breath, please do ask me some questions!" Yab finished, charismatically, as it was only natural of his personality. "We will take one question from the judges," the announcer said and it read, "Plant-based foods have been around for quite some time–not to mention chili peppers and spices–so where is the disruption?"

"Aha!" Yab exclaimed, "I was expecting this at some point. You see, due to demand increase from younger generations while mass immigration brings in new dishes, plant-based foods have become a billion-dollar industry worldwide. And when it comes to peppers, the heat level is merely the tip of the iceberg, since there is so much more to it than what meets the eye. In fact, back home, we have taken a whole different approach to it. Flavor and natural color are our primary focus at this point. We now work with dozens of species that differ in taste, from floral to fruity and smoky to sweet! We can custom-grow over thirty varieties of peppers varying in color, heat, and aroma!"

Yab smiled, more confident about his idea than ever before.

"Chili peppers are literally the hottest ingredient in the culinary industry, and let me explain why!" Yab exclaimed with passion. "I have worked at a restaurant since my arrival in the US. Two out of three clients requested a plant-based alternative. For younger consumers, meat is overrated, and plant-based brands are, little by little, coming up with a complete variety of delicious and attractive food options. There are even some plant-based "meats" that taste better than the original burger patties. In addition, as more people recognize the ills of meat consumption; plant proteins, mixed up with the appropriate spices and chili peppers as the final touch, are excellent candidates to substitute it." With this, Yab took a long sip of water, indicating that he was done talking.

"Any closing remarks, Yab?"

"Well…there is one final thing I'd like to add. Actually, my speech wouldn't feel complete without it," Yab said, in a shy voice. "After living in the US and getting the chance to experience the American Dream up close, I felt my roots to Copán stronger than ever. Therefore, I must add that all this plan comes from my desire to create stronger ties between these two worlds.

"We want to go that extra mile to assure consumers that if they buy Spice Society products, they'll only receive the *best* products. Final consumers are as important to the business equation as our farmers and our clients…because, let's face it: without loyal and continuous market demand, there simply is no Spice Society. Therefore, I invite all of my listeners to join The Spice Society: A friendly food community that looks out for each other's interests…changing food and changing the world. Thank you very much!"

The judges seemed pleased and intrigued by Yab's passion and determination. The audience applauded, and the announcer stood there shocked by the eloquent speech Yab had delivered. It wasn't every day that someone so passionate took the stage. And Yab was that person because he believed every word, not for the money, but for the impact he could make.

They excused Yab for a few moments until the judges made their final decision.

Yab stood backstage with the spinner in his hand. Irrespective of what happened now, he was satisfied with his performance. "Thank you, Abuelo," Yab murmured to himself. "You taught me so much. Even if I fail now, I know it's going to be a stepping stone to something greater. I can see my goal clearly now–it's as vivid as the macaws–and it's mostly thanks to you, Abuelo. Thank you!"

Fifteen minutes went by…very…slowly…

"And the winner is…" the announcer exclaimed from the stage, building anticipation. Drum roll, please…THE SPICE SOCIETY!" The announcer called Yab up for him to give a few words and get his picture taken.

15

THE OFFICIAL START-UP MAGAZINE

The night of victory was hosted by Phil and his team, with a beautiful night of drinks while discussing the venture and what Yab's next steps would be. Phil booked him a room in a nice hotel and told him that he had a surprise for the next day.

The morning came, and Yab slept blissfully for the first time in months, in a proper bed, with a proper breakfast and a warm shower.

The phone rang, and Phil asked Yab to join him in the hotel's lobby. Phil also mentioned to Yab that his assistant would bring him a suit. Yab grew curious about where this was going. He wore the suit and found Phil in the hotel's café, sitting with a woman, chatting.

"There he is," Phil said with a proud smile and a quick wink. "Let me introduce Nicole Shawn, a journalist for the event's official start-up magazine."

"Pleasure to meet you, Yab," Nicole said, and they exchanged a handshake.

Nicole is here to make your profile for the event's magazine," Phil explained.

"We do this with all the winners and the runners-up," Nicole added.

Phil leaned back, letting Yab and Nicole talk, observing the interview in silence. She grabbed her recorder from her bag and placed it on the table.

"Are you interested in answering a few questions?" Nicole asked.

Yab only nodded. He had never been interviewed before. And to go from that to now getting interviewed for the competition's magazine, to inspire the next generations of entrepreneurs…He could barely smile, more anxious than he was happy.

They went on with questions about Yab's early life, and Yab didn't miss the opportunity to mention his family and his Abuelo. They talked about the plant-based chicken origins and his previous attempts as an entrepreneur, and they ended with the most important questions of all.

"So, Yab, let's get to the one question that most young entrepreneurs are dying to hear you answer: How did someone starting from scratch make it this far; all the way back from a local chicken restaurant–"or pollera" as it's called back where you're from–to crossing the border illegally to working with a venture capital investment firm? How in the world did you get here?"

"You'd be surprised, but it's a combination of factors that I realized recently have acted in my favor," Yab said with a clear smile, remembering all he had been through. "Everything played its part for me to end up here."

"I'm all ears," Nicole said.

"It all started with this," said Yab, placing the beautiful spinner on the table.

"My Abuelo, the wisest man I know, taught me how to manifest."

"What does that mean?"

Yab went over the Spinner and explained to Nicole how the sun represented one's internal dialogue. He went on to summarize that the stars represented a person's goals and that these should generate powerful emotions through words–as vivid as the macaw parrots–so they can finally activate the creative mind's holcan.

"Very interesting. Did your Abuelo come up with this technique?" Nicole asked.

"He learned it from his ancestors," Yab confirmed.

"What other experiences helped you in your journey, Yab?"

Yab looked back on the challenges, the opportunities, and how he handled every obstacle in his way. It hadn't been an easy journey. He learned more in these past five years than he had in his entire life. There was a single common factor in all his experiences, Yab realized. Looking back, the spinner gave him courage, but his mindset pushed him forward.

"There is another important factor," Yab added. "I want to call it the growth mindset," he said.

"What exactly do you mean?" Nicole asked.

"It's very simple, really. It's an attitude made up of small things that allow a real inner and outward transformation," Yab said and thought for a moment. "First, we need to embrace challenges, viewing each challenge as a chance to grow and looking at conflict as an opportunity to become better. With that in mind, we need to persist in the face of setbacks."

"What type of setbacks?" Nicole asked.

"Many things–from the lack of having a stable job to family issues and failed businesses. I've faced many hardships, but I never stopped trying. I've always tried to solve the problems before me; I've never given up," Yab said. Eventually, the warrior in me comes up with a creative solution every time."

"That's a very valuable lesson," Nicole said.

Yab smiled. "Thirdly, I have seen *effort* as a path toward mastery, not as a fruitless action, even when I 'fail'. I have always thought that my endeavors would one day reward me, and today I can say that even the simplest things in my life have contributed to my being here."

"That's truly beautiful," Nicole said.

"Other important tools are learning to accept feedback instead of rejecting it and seeing others' success as an inspiration and an opportunity to work harder–to shoot for the stars! Now that I think about it, I've applied these principles throughout my entire life, and they have never failed me. They became second nature to me, and today I can fully appreciate what they'll help me become."

"So, you've just given away your secret recipe to success?" Nicole asked playfully. "If any other entrepreneur follows these steps, then he should surely succeed?"

Yab responded with friendly laughter. "Haha! I don't think it's as simple as following a recipe; I'd rather say that they are principles that worked for me, and I believe they'll help any other determined entrepreneur along his journey!" Yab held on to what he was going to say next and thought for a minute. "There's something else, though," he finally said. Something that not everyone is blessed enough to have but can definitely choose to give to the next generations," Yab said.

"Do tell!" Nicole exclaimed.

"Well, I come from a very blessed family, and not everyone has had this gift, but anyone can give it to their own family; it's never too late. Ever since I was a kid, I have been supported by my parents and my Abuelo. They didn't lie to me or exaggerate, but they have never failed to inspire and affirm my efforts and hard work. Back then, I didn't realize that they were working on building a strong internal dialogue in me. It's helped me realize that when I speak to others, it should only be words of encouragement and not of dismay that can put down anyone's dreams–much like my family did with me, always supporting me to spread my wings and fly!"

"This is very hard to incorporate into our lives, but it works! Even though I might be far away from my loved ones, I can still hear their voices inside my mind, guiding me and blessing me."

Nicole was pleased with the thorough interview. "You'll be an inspiration to future generations, Yab," Nicole said. "I'm sure of it."

"If I may add something here," Phil said, coming in all of the sudden.

"Of course," Nicole said, turning the recorder his way. "What does the benefactor have to say about all that?"

"Just a man with good vision," said Phil. "Just a man who saw an opportunity to give back by investing in a bright idea."

Nicole took a note of that.

"Yab is a top-notch example of the heart and passion an immigrant should have in the US. Yab isn't thinking only about himself and his own well-being but pursuing good for the people around him and his people back home. We always talk about immigrants occupying important jobs in the US, but the discussion should also consider how, in many cases, immigrants *create* job opportunities for people in their home countries.

"Let's create the American dream in the immigrants' countries of origin! It's people like Yab who manage to be this bridge, which brings the best of two worlds together. It's a moral duty for us entrepreneurs to create economic opportunities that wouldn't be otherwise available for the disadvantaged collectives, and I know that one connection at a time, we can certainly achieve such a task. As they say, there's no better way to fight crime than a good job or education.

"Of course, the world is separated by many factors, but we can choose whether to view them as divisions or as an opportunity for connection. Instead of acting individually and independently, we could choose to act collectively and mutualistically; the world would be filled with incredible platforms such as Spice Society, but we frequently fail to act on these opportunities."

"What do you mean by that?" asked Nicole. "Mutualistic how?"

"What I mean is, we can choose to trust these small growers to help us scale our plant-based foods while improving their lives. We'll build a connection with Central America: We improve our plant-based products, and they increase production and job opportunities. This is mutualism. *Symbiosis*."

Nicole took frantic notes. Yab knew all of Phil's views on the world and immigration, but listening to his talk, Yab felt awe for being a part of this.

"Lastly, I want to call for our political leadership to incorporate this requirement into the immigration policy. Every immigrant, regardless of their limitations, education, or opportunities, should commit to creating a project to help their countries back home, and this can take many forms, in different areas–not only trade. Health, education–you name it. ICE should follow up on this commitment, and perhaps by doing so, we will begin tackling the true root cause of immigration. We might begin improving the living conditions in our hemisphere and become the good neighbors we were always meant to be."

"Thank you," Nicole said. "You have a very interesting stance on the immigration problem."

"But remember…" Yab locked his eyes with Nicole's.

"…It is not a problem," Phil added. "…It's an opportunity!"

The interview concluded with a few parting words from Nicole, leaving Yab and Phil behind to discuss their next steps and the future of their partnership.

16

THE SPICE SOCIETY

As soon as the challenge was over, with all the expenses covered by the venture competition, Yab took a six-month trip around the world to research and learn about the origins of spices, chili peppers, and plant-based proteins. His trip started in the US, then took him through Africa and Europe, the Middle East, Asia, and finally back to Latin America.

Being a cook and knowing that the source of his fire and success was creating dishes that people would love ensured that Yab never lost the consumer perspective; whenever he analyzed a new recipe combination, he made sure it was healthy, flavorful, and trendy.

Yab had the opportunity to meet and build relationships with local producers, farmers, and other food manufacturers around the globe. He visited many native restaurants and tried various home-grown, plant-based dishes.

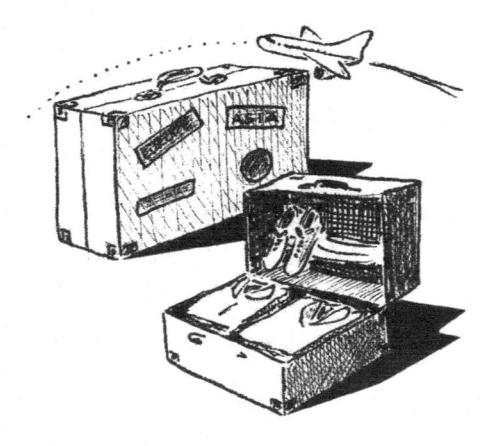

Although based on his original objectives Yab had already succeeded, he had realized that success was more an attitude and a process than a destination, so he kept re-writing his vivid goals to adapt them to each of the stages of his life, and his wish of helping others was evermore alive. As he boarded a flight and prepared to depart for the next destination, he would revise and recite his mantra, which by now had evolved yet again:

"I embrace that the world is flat and can do business anywhere, and I create a platform that develops abundance for thousands of farmers back home, making families happy across the globe as they enjoy and share delicious, organic, and healthy ingredients."

With a notepad always in hand, Yab took notes, jotted down information, tips, and best practices on health and wellness. He canvassed the global market, assessing the needs, demands, and unique farming practices of other cultures, which inevitably led him to grow as a chef, as a businessman, and as a person; his early life struggles and hard efforts were starting to pay off.

Yab always kept one of his father's coffee industry quotes in his heart:

"Always try to learn," his father used to say. "There's always something new to discover–better techniques to find. If you feel that you have nothing else to learn, then you have already lost, my son."

And that's what Yab did. This trip was not to self-validate his success. This trip was to learn from shared experiences and to anticipate how he could serve the customer better with the healthiest, most delicious trends in the world.

• • •

After six months of intense traveling, Yab finally went back home to his beautiful Copán, grinning ear to ear when he saw the picturesque view of the town.

His family and friends were waiting for him at the airport, his father standing among them with his chest puffed and a wide smile of pride and respect splashed on his face. The welcoming hug brought warmth into Yab's heart. He was finally home, amongst friends and family again. Tears overwhelmed his eyes, and as he pulled his loved ones in closer, Yab finally spoke: "I'm so happy to see you! I did this all for you. All of you. None of it would have even been possible without you affirming me and supporting me all those years... Thank you, guys!

They drove back home, and they had a lavish dinner with one dish after the other. Everyone pitched in, and they all cooked together. Yab had missed this. The simplicity of a family dinner where everyone from the neighboring houses brought plates of their food and contributed to the abundance laid on the table.

Everyone was eager to listen to stories from the US, and sparing no detail, Yab told them everything that had happened in the past few years, while he was away. Of course, he had stayed in touch with his family and friends, but that wasn't the same as talking to them in person while laughing together, crying together, and teasing one another.

After the dinner was over, Yab sat in the garden, with a local beer in his hand, for the first time appreciating how good it tasted. It all began here, at this table and bench, dreaming big with Dominic.

Now their dreams seemed small–childish even. The plant-based nuggets were a nice idea, but it wasn't enough for Yab. *The government program can keep the formula,* Yab thought. He now had something better in his hands: resilience.

"You made us all proud, you know," his father grabbed a seat across from Yab and raised his bottle of beer as if making a toast with nothing but a gesture.

"You shouldn't be drinking beer," Yab said.

"Don't tell your mother," his dad giggled with eyes wide open and placed his finger on his lips, begging for Yab's silence. The doctor said I can't drink coffee, eat fried food, and that I should cut back on the meat, so spoil your old man and let it be our little secret, will you?"

Yab laughed, in solidarity with his old man. "Don't worry, Dad," Yab reassured him. "Now that I'm back, I'll cook a plant-based chicken burger for you, and it will be so tasty that you won't be able to tell the difference. I guarantee it!"

"Thank God, because your mother has lost some of her cooking magic," his father said.

They shared a laugh and toasted, clicking the glasses together.

"I'm sorry that I wasn't here for so long, Dad," Yab finally said.

It was the only thing that weighed him down over the years. The fact that he never came to visit his father, even when he was in the hospital.

"Are you kidding me?" his father said, growing serious. "If it wasn't for you, my boy, we wouldn't have been able to pay all those bills! Don't take this the wrong way, but you blessed us by staying there, and I'm deeply grateful, Son. I'm proud of the man you've become, you should know that!"

"Thank you, Dad," Yab said. "Still, if I had listened to your advice, I could have stayed here and maybe succeed without having to go through all that I did."

"What advice?" his father asked.

"That everything I need is here," Yab said. "It was right after all. What we needed was plants, local groceries, food, and farmers from Central America. I traveled all the way to the US to realize that success wasn't over there, Dad, but right here, in our dear and blessed Mayan lands."

"As much as I want to take credit for that..." His father raised a sly smile. "Your Abuelo is the one who used to say that all the time. These weren't words of my making."

"He didn't say anything about it when I visited him," Yab said.

"Maybe he wanted you to face this challenge," his father said. "When you left, your Abuelo said that he wanted you to stay here. He was afraid for your life even. But he trusted you, and he knew how important this trip would be for your future. He was like you one day, traveling around the world, meeting people, doing things. That's how he became the man that he is today! Be thankful you have had such a powerful mentor in life, Yab."

"I am, Dad, but not just for Abuelo. You and mom have always been there for me too. I talked about you in the magazine interview," Yab said.

"I'm famous now?" his father asked jokingly while making a funny gesture and holding his chest.

They shared a laugh once again.

"Let's go," his father said, emptying his coffee. "You have a lot to do, don't you?"

"Yes, but it can wait. Family is more important," Yab said.

"Nonsense," his father said. "We'll be here tomorrow and the day after that, cheering for your success and comforting you with your losses! Go and seize the world, my boy."

With a friendly pat on the back, his dad went inside the house, leaving Yab alone, who set his sights again upon the beautiful fields of Copán. He took a deep breath, smelling the peppers, the wet mud, and the fragrances in the air.

"I'm glad I'm home…"

• • •

Yab didn't spend any of the competition prize money until it was time to start his business. Phil had flown from the US, and together, they started working on the business' details. With Yab's know-how regarding local agriculture and Phil's business experience, the two started working on setting up a greenhouse, a stockpile plant, and administrative offices; Yab's goals slowly turned from ideas to reality.

Yab found the perfect spot for his headquarters, a place close to the plantations but with enough room for expansion and growth. And Yab couldn't believe his eyes when he looked across the street, through the window of his new office. He took this as a sign of confirmation from above, and his heart was filled with happiness and peace. For there was a ceiba tree. It took him at least half an hour of silence to properly assimilate the meaning of the situation: he simply decided to be grateful to God for such a lovely "coincidence."

It would take a few good months to recruit a management team and for the offices to be prepared, but Yab and Phil didn't wait. Yab had to pave the ground for what was to come, and their next step was the most vital one: gaining the skeptic farmers' trust and persuading them to join The Spice Society.

Phil returned to the US to work on distribution with the help of his team, to meet with potential clients, and to ensure the demand of the Spice Society's supply chain.

Yab started with the first expert farmers he already knew to be extremely reliable. He visited their plantations one by one, explaining his idea to them.

Yab visited an old friend first…Don Constantino, a respectable farmer in the area with a large family of devoted chili producers. Don Constantino invited Yab to his house where the meeting would take place.

"Yab, my friend," Don Constantino said from the porch when Yab arrived.

"Don Constantino!" Yab replied.

"I heard about you and your victory at the competition," Don Constantino said. "Your mother came to visit us. She wouldn't stop talking about you."

"She is really proud, yes," Yab said.

"Come on inside," Don Constantino said invitingly. "Do you want a beer?"

"Yes, please."

The two sat in Don Constantino's backyard with a full view of the entire plantation.

"So, what brings you here?" he asked with curious eyes.

"I came back because I'm starting a sustainable Agro company," Yab said.

"Ah, your father mentioned something about spices," Don Constantino said.

"Exactly," Yab said. "But not only spices. I'd like to focus on plant-based proteins too! And I want us to work together like we did with the plant-based chicken nuggets".

"I am humbled," said Don Constantino, bowing his head. "So, what's the great idea?"

"You've known me for quite some time, from when I was a baby, really," Yab said. "And you know I've always dreamed of making a big contribution to our community, right?"

"Right." Don Constantino took a sip from his beer. "You've had some great ideas over the years."

"Now, a shift in international consumer demand is on our side," Yab said and smiled, passion oozing from every word.

Don Constantino leaned forward, attracted by Yab's passion.

"You see, so far, you've worked growing and selling crops to local buyers, right?"

"Yes."

"What if I told you that we could do better than selling locally and triple your output?" Yab asked.

"Did you just say *triple?*" Don Constantino asked in disbelief, "Wait…but what's wrong with the way things are now anyways? My father always said that it's madness to change what already works!"

"Well, I wouldn't say that something is necessarily wrong; all I'm saying is that things could be better…way better. I want us to form a sustainable export community!

"Currently, amongst the main buyers, there are plenty of national companies that take advantage of their dominant position when dealing with the farming community. They don't care about the long-term stability of the collaboration or of the long-term wellbeing of your community. I want to change that: I want you to work *with* me, not for me. I don't want to come, buy your products, and then just leave," Yab said. I care about my region and about the people in it. "We can work together, and I can help you progress: to have integrated pest management methods in place, safe crop protection practices, and drip irrigation, and I'll make sure that your product always sells!"

"Ah, wait a second, Yab," Don Constantino said. "You can't promise all that and expect me to believe it. Even the big family businesses and corporations around here fail and sometimes don't want to buy our crops; what makes you better?"

"First, I'll make sure that we'll export to the US. The demand there is high, and because of their natural climate they can't grow all the crops that we can here," Yab said. "And we won't focus only on chilis. I'll help you diversify your field and cultivate all types of plant-based foods! Don Constantino, when you now walk into a supermarket in the US, it's amazing to see the variety of options that exist. There are new vegan categories of everything: refrigerated milk, frozen desserts, and meat. Can you believe they are selling plant-based chicken in the US? For us, its composition is as common as bread, but they view it as something extraordinary! To them, it's not just a cheap food solution; it's a revolution!

They are actively trying to reduce meat consumption. It's not like here, where it's a matter of necessity. It's a growing trend, and it will keep on growing due to health and wellness. This plant revolution is transforming into big business for retailers and manufacturers alike, and it's farmers like us that will source the freshest ingredients, which are all made from plants–the same ones that you and I are used to growing. I'll show you all of the agricultural research and development we've been able to develop so that we can compete worldwide."

Don Constantino frowned. "But tradition dictates that we are chili pepper growers. That's what we know how to do. My father and father's father all devoted their lives to chilis. You want me to change things now? It just doesn't feel right, my boy."

Yab smiled.

"You are right. You are right, my friend," Yab said. "But answer me this: How many times has the price of crops come down because of sudden local overproduction?"

Don Constantino thought about it for a moment, and Yab continued.

"How many times have you been forced to throw away a part of your production? Aren't you tired of living amidst the uncertainty of whether or not you'll make it to the month's end?

"I don't want you to change what you believe in and make you take blind risks," Yab said. "I want us to take it slow, understand the scope and potential of the proposal, and I'll show you how we can both profit and grow together! If we just added cashews, black-eyed peas, and lupini beans–all very high in proteins–you would have better-diversified crops to sell year-round. We would still have a high demand for chili peppers and I'll make sure these continue to sell, as they are complementary to the demand in plant-based meat!"

"You did your research, didn't you?" Don Constantino asked with a proud smile. "Changing the plantation now requires money! We don't have that kind of money."

"I told you I want us to work together," Yab said, smiling: "We will do that together. And I have found a few new processes that can increase your annual yield–three times what you had last year with little to no expenses!

"What processes?" Don Constantino asked. "We know how to farm. Our methods are traditional and ensure the best results!"

"We will not alter the way you do things, we'll simply provide the resources to make it better! With seed technology, plant density, and drip irrigation, you'll see tremendous results." Yab claimed, excitedly. "I will give you all of the seeds and you will be able to partner up with co-ops for asset investments and we will secure and oversee your relationship with them."

Don Constantino thought about it: the co-op's machines he had always thought of but never taken the risk of buying. He met Yab's passionate, confident eyes. His preparation was solid and Yab sure brought good arguments to the table. No one could deny that Yab knew what he was talking about, and Don Constantino felt safe in Yab's presence. Seeing a man he knew and loved, Don Constantino decided to join Yab's endeavor.

"But if it doesn't work out, we will go back to what we know, okay?" Don Constantino said.

"Of course. If it doesn't work out, I'll make sure never to bother you again, but trust me, we will have a durable commercial relationship; you won't be able to get rid of me easily," Yab finished with a friendly chuckle.

They shook hands and Don Constantino promised to persuade some of the other farmers as well. It would be better if they heard it from another farmer. They celebrated their newly created collaboration by making a toast.

With a respectable farmer and upstanding member of their community such as Don Constantino at their side, more farmers started to join Spice Society. Yab's plan and promises inspired them, not only for the better working conditions, but for the prospect of a transparent, honest collaboration, and it seemed like a good strategy for the region and the country as a whole.

Once again, farmers started to group together and Spice Society began to form, Yab upheld his promise. He arranged a meeting with a team of experts to educate the farmers and help them prepare the new year's yields. The farmers listened to the experts enthusiastically, smiling at the prospect of producing larger yields, with less effort, and less risk. Despite the year's misfortunes and hardships, the farmers seemed eager, infused once again with purpose and dedication to their craft, all thanks to Yab. He visited the plantations daily, discussing details with the farmers, taking notes about their complaints and reservations, and analyzing what could be improved. They started working together as a family: Holding meetings where they discussed and learned from each other, improving not only as businessmen and farmers but as people and most importantly, as a society!

Soon enough, Yab had established the cornerstone of Spice Society–the first good farmers to work alongside him. Yet, the obstacle he'd overcome was only the first of many. They had a long journey before them, with many decisions to be made and many loose ends to be tied. And Yab was more than excited for what the future held for him. He didn't falter at the challenges; he smiled at the idea that this was just the beginning. Spice Society's story was just unfolding.

• • •

As the first quarter came to a close, over a dozen plantations had already joined The Spice Society. The brand-new offices were finally operative, full of Phil's people taking care of the day-to-day logistics, marketing, and accounting tasks; coordinating the entire effort.

Yab arrived at the office early in the morning, as he did every day, and prepared for his first big video conference with Phil. Today would be the first recap of the quarter, to evaluate their growth, goals met, and actionable steps from that point on.

The video came on, and Yab greeted Phil. He seemed troubled, and a little tired, as if he had been up all night.

"Let's begin," Phil said, cutting right to the chase. "I have some good news and some bad news."

Yab's smile faded. He thought everything was moving along smoothly, as planned. "Let's start with the good news," Yab said.

Phil moved around sheets and stacks of paper, going through the reports his team had collected over the past few months, studying them meticulously. "Okay, so the few plantations you managed to recruit are generating more local revenue than we anticipated," Phil said. "It's looking good. There are already a few potential investors and buyers for us, so there's definitely hope for Spice Society."

"This is amazing," Yab said. "What's the bad news then?"

"It's not enough." Phil shot a tired look at the camera. "While the few plantations exceed our expectations, overall, things are not as hopeful as we originally expected. We are growing in size, but based on our original plan, we should have had double the profits by now. There have been plenty of unforeseen costs that have come up, though."

"I see," Yab said and frowned. "But it's a good thing that the few plantations generate more than we expected."

"It certainly is, but the goals we set were pretty conservative already. They were goals to judge Spice Society's potential," Phil explained. "If we don't meet those goals by the end of the year, I'm afraid that Spice Society will be over. The potential investors and businesses won't be persuaded by the numbers."

"What are we going to do, then?" Yab said with a sense of dread forming.

"We'll have to find a way to attract more farmers," Phil said, skimming through the reports, "it's either that or we won't have the critical mass required to be profitable."

The same hesitations that Don Constantino had were holding back other farmers as well, and many of them were far more reluctant. There were more than a few farmers that didn't want to join Spice Society. Out of stubbornness, fear of change, and respect for their traditional ways, the old farmers rejected Yab's proposition, sticking to what they knew. Without the older and more experienced farmers, it was natural that many younger ones would refuse the offer as well.

Yab started pacing back and forth. "They're just comfortable with their current way of doing things. Some of them don't even want to hear what I have to say," Yab grumbled. "As soon as I call, they act as if they know what I want to suggest and decline immediately."

"Isn't there a way to attract them? There must be something that they want," Phil said. "You know these people better than I do. That's why I'm trusting your leadership in this."

"I think they need a motive," Yab said, thinking out loud. "A better cause than the one they already have. Something intriguing enough to force them to rethink their choices."

Yab sat back behind his desk, grabbing the spinner and fiddling with it as he always did when presented with a tough challenge.

"I wish we could offer more money, but that would defeat the purpose," Phil said.

"I don't think it's about the money," Yab objected. "They know they'll earn more eventually. Don Constantino is proof of that." Yab gave the spinner another go…

"And we can't just let them stick with their old ways," Phil said. "That would defeat one of the core purposes of Spice Society."

Yab nodded and looked at the spinner as it slowly came to a halt. The symbols were visible once again, and Yab's gaze finally rested on the Mayan star. Remembering his Abuelo's goal-setting advice, he sat up with a jolt. "Of course!" Yab exclaimed with a smile. "How did we miss that?"

Phil shot him a questioning look.

"I think I know what we can do," Yab said and picked up the phone.

About an hour later, Yab's Abuelo stepped inside the conference room. Yab introduced Phil to Abuelo.

"It's an honor to meet you," Phil said. "Yab speaks highly of you!"

"And of you," Abuelo said. "It's good to know that my grandson has finally found a partner worthy of his good character!"

"You are too nice, Abuelo," Yab said, going straight to the point: "Okay, Phil, as you know, my Abuelo is a respectable figure in the region," Yab explained.

"Yab, now you're the one exaggerating," said Abuelo, humble as always.

"Now is not the time to be modest, Abuelo," Yab said. "I want to ask you to give a speech to the co-op about Spice Society. If you believe in the idea, they will too, or at least, reconsider it!"

"I do believe in the idea very much," Abuelo said.

"That's a great idea, Yab," Phil exclaimed. "Let me know when the presentation will take place, and I'll be there."

"What do you say, Abuelo?" Yab asked.

"Anything I can do to help," said Abuelo, flashing a warm smile.

They spent the better part of the day planning Abuelo's speech, but Abuelo already seemed prepared–as usual. He had spent his entire life here, amongst those people, helping and interacting with them. Wise as he was, Abuelo understood Spice Society's purpose, and he had the right arguments for the local farmers.

"I have another meeting with a plantation owner today," Yab said. "I have to go. Now, the only thing left to do is to schedule a meeting with the co-op. They didn't even want to hear me out last time I tried to approach them."

"We'll figure something out," Abuelo said. "Do you want me to attend today's meeting with you?"

"That would be great, Abuelo," Yab said. "That way we get our gears turning already".

Yab and his Abuelo left the offices for a plantation up north. On their way there, Yab was anxious, but he didn't know why. He hadn't felt this anxious during the meetings with the other farmers.

Upon their arrival in the mountainous sanctuary, Yab saw many familiar faces, proud farmers, all enjoying refreshments to battle the day's heat. Many turned their attention to Yab's Abuelo, greeting him, inviting him over for a drink and to talk, as they always loved to discuss high ideas and difficult concepts with Abuelo.

Inspecting the crowd of farmers, Yab realized where his anxiety was coming from.

Among the familiar faces, Dominic stepped hesitantly toward Yab, head hunched and a guilty expression plastered across his face.

"Dominic," Yab said. "I expected to see you here."

Dominic remained silent, barely able to look Yab in the eye. He worked his jaw, trying to say something, but no words came out of his mouth.

"How's your family?" Yab asked.

"Listen Yab, I never had a chance to apologize, Yab," Dominic said. "I never wanted things to end the way they did. It's just that…"

Yab remained silent. He didn't want to dwell on the past and revisit the pain Dominic had caused him, but it would be rude not to let him explain himself and apologize.

Dominic hesitated. He raised his head, staring at Yab's distant expression. Yab wanted to forgive him, but it was easier said than done. Just looking at Dominic, Yab felt the same pain he experienced when he discovered that Dominic had stolen his recipe and cut Yab out from the profits.

A bitter expression carved Dominic's face. Bitter not from envy but from guilt for betraying his old friend.

"Man, please forgive me!" Dominic said in a stronger and more desperate tone. "How stupid I was to act the way I did; to tell you the truth, I wasn't prepared to see you again, but I do know I'm deeply sorry.

"I had some time to reflect after you left Copán, and I couldn't stop thinking that it was my fault you had to leave. I kept thinking about your trip to the US–how hard it must have been. If anything had happened to you, I couldn't have forgiven myself."

Abuelo was staring at Yab with a face that spoke louder than words. His eyes suggested that Yab forgive, reminding him that he came from a compassionate family.

"Look, what you did was inexcusable," Yab said. "If we would have talked it out beforehand, like partners, I might have been open to exploring the idea of selling, or at least trusting your insight."

"I know," Dominic said, his gaze returning to the floor.

"I don't think we can be business partners ever again after that," Yab said. "It will take a lot of work for me to trust you again, but we can start out fresh for the good of the community. You're still one of the leaders of your co-op right?"

"Yes, I returned to farming. Things didn't work out for me as they did for you," Dominic said.

"I can help," Yab said. "I want you to be a part of Spice Society!"

Dominic was at a loss for words. His jaw dropped, and his eyes widened.

"After what I did, you still want my help?" Dominic asked.

"You are just a victim of the system and what you see around you, as was I," Yab said. "I want to change that. After all, if you hadn't crossed me back then, we wouldn't have The Spice Society today!"

"I didn't expect this kind of proposition," Dominic said. "I heard you were recruiting, but I didn't think I would be a part of this."

"I'm not recruiting," Yab said. "I'm inviting you. Spice Society is a family and we can always use more members. You'll keep running your co-op the same way you do now, but you'll be working with me as well. But no funny business this time. If I sense that something's wrong, I won't hesitate to cut you loose."

Yab spread his hand forward for a firm business handshake. "What do you say? Are you in?"

Dominic's smile, hesitant but full of relief, returned. "Anything you need from me, I'll help you, any way that I can!" Dominic said. "You won't regret this!"

"We have only one problem that we need help with for now," Yab said.

"Anything you need," Dominic said emphatically.

"We want our family to grow. We want more members–more farmers–to improve not only our family but Copán as a whole," Yab said. "But you know how these farmers are. Most of the members refuse to even hear us out. We need to find a way to persuade them–especially those members of the main co-op".

"I think I have a few ideas," Dominic said.

"I just want you to schedule a meeting with the other leaders," Yab said, still hesitant about Dominic's involvement in Spice Society.

It was one thing to have Dominic working his plantation, and it was another to let him make decisions and suggest ideas. Yab wanted to give him the benefit of the doubt, but Dominic had a long way to go before proving his loyalty again.

"That I can do," Dominic said. "Consider it done!"

"Thank you, Dominic," Yab said.

Despite the obviousness of Yab's need for help, it was written all over Dominic's face, he couldn't believe that Yab was willing to give him a chance.

And so their collaboration began anew.

During that brief meeting, Abuelo took the lead first, and then Dominic pitched in with a few encouraging words for his former friend. Yab's presentation and arguments, backed by the introduction of the other two, managed to seal the deal. A handful of farmers joined Spice Society; a sign that the family would keep on growing.

17

WHITE SMOKE

Thanks to Dominic's efforts and influence in the farmers' circles, Yab managed to schedule a meeting with the leaders of the main co-op, who finally agreed to see him and hear his case. Dominic advised Yab that many had already agreed to reject the offer, but Yab would nonetheless make the most of this opportunity. Even if the farmers were adamant, Yab had to make the best presentation possible. He wouldn't give up without a fight.

Yab, Abuelo, and Phil had reached the fields outside Copán and were now sitting in a small cafe where the leaders liked to spend their time after a hard day's work. Under the day's heat, the streets were empty, and even the breeze brought more heat.

Yab was anxious, constantly rubbing his sweaty palms against his pants, adjusting his clothes, fixing his hair. His breathing was fast. This meeting was key to Spice Society's success. This co-operative grouped six hundred small landowners of the area, every one of them important, a vital component of Spice Society's future. If these farmers agreed to join Yab's family, it would open the doors to the goals that he and Phil had been planning all this time. If the meeting was a success, they could begin operations with two thousand producers, which would serve as a reference for other regions in Central America.

Phil had already secured a few prospects waiting in the US, and Yab felt like everyone's eyes were on Spice Society by now. If this meeting went badly, they would probably have to abandon the Spice Society dream or work even harder for many more months to recover.

Abuelo turned with serene eyes and a peaceful smile, not a single hint of worry in his features. "Why are you so nervous?" Abuelo asked.

"You know how much this meeting means to us," Yab said. "We can't afford for it to go badly."

Abuelo placed his hand on Yab's shoulder, a gesture that seemed to cure Yab of the anxiety. It was as if Abuelo's positive energy flowed right through him.

"These people–they can be stubborn, yes, but they are business-savvy," Abuelo said. "You have a wonderful idea here, Yab, and only a stupid man would turn it down."

"I hope you're right," Yab said as they approached the door.

"I already know what to say to them," Abuelo said after a brief silence.

Yab opened the door and entered the steaming-hot cafe where all the leaders were seated around the room; a few rounds of coffee had already been served while waiting for Yab and his Abuelo. The room went silent as soon as Yab stepped inside, and all eyes turned to the door.

Yab greeted the leaders properly.

"Good afternoon, my friends. My name is Yab, this is my associate Phil, and here's my Abuelo, who many of you already know," Yab said. "Thank you for agreeing to meet with us. We'll be brief, as we don't want to take too much of your time."

Yab and Phil grabbed a seat as Abuelo walked, stick in hand, to the middle of the room and greeted everyone by their first names. He was frail with the curved posture common to those of his advanced age–a visage that instilled love in anyone who saw him. Despite never having ventured into politics due to all of the corruption, this was a man that many times had gathered the leaders of the town to help solve important challenges. They respected him and perhaps even felt peace in his presence. He was a man that always managed to draw the interest of the people around him, and he quickly became the soul of every crowd without ever saying much.

Abuelo cleared his throat and started with his warm, caring, and positive voice. "My old friends, neighbors, countrymen, and women, I'm very happy to be here with you," he said and gave his signature chuckle. It was evident that Abuelo really enjoyed being part of the project's discussion, almost as if he had missed being part of something bigger for a long time.

"Today I'm not here to pursue one of my 'crazy ideas' as you might have called them in the past, but I'm here to vouch for my grandson," Abuelo continued. "One of the finest men I have ever known and one that I am deeply proud of. I assure you, I wouldn't say any of that if I didn't mean it. You know me; I don't spare the truth and always employ candor with all of you, so please remember that my words have no bias. I truly believe in this young man, and I want to help you see what I see."

The leaders and farmers of the audience nodded, smiling encouragingly. They always loved to listen to the old man speak, and they all agreed that he was a man of honor and principle, who never sugar-coated anything.

"We are here today to invite you to be pioneers in creating what we call the American Dream…but from here in Central America!"

The coop leaders were bemused. Their eyes were impressed and confused. Yab could almost sense their thoughts: What was the old man up to now? He was famous for his list of crazy ideas–making Copán a world heritage site, AIDS prevention, and making the macaws fly again…all of which he had achieved in one lifetime.

Since his Abuelo was always living in his small farm near the ruins, people never found his ideas opportunistic and never saw any foul play in his incentives. He was always honest and never pursued money, something that intrigued them even more.

Noticing the strange looks in the farming community's faces, like a trained orator, Abuelo continued with an explanation. "Allow me to speak in terms familiar to all of us. How many more sons, daughters, and grandchildren do we have to see leave the country and break our hearts in pursuit of a better future?"

"And we all know that this is the less tragic scenario! But how many more *funerals* will we have to endure? How many more of those horrendous phone calls in the middle of the night, asking us to come down to the police station to identify the corpse that used to carry the soul of our son or daughter? Hundreds of families lose their children on their journey to the US, and I know that some of you have experienced this terrible fate. Most of you are old like me, and you all know that no parent should bury their children! This cannot become a Central American tradition. I cannot accept that."

Many somber looks came from the crowd. People were hurt and frustrated, aching at the thought of immigration–how their children kept on leaving. It was a story relatable to all of them. Even Yab felt the pain, remembering what he'd been forced to go through.

"My grandson could have lost his life on the trip to the US if not for the grace of God," said Abuelo, pointing at Yab. "And this young man could have lost his soul if not for his mental fortitude, resilience, and hard work. I prayed every day and every night for his safety, but that's not a life that any of us want, is it?"

More somber nods came from the crowd, which now was hanging from Abuelo's lips.

"Our country isn't perfect, I know that," Abuelo said. "Crony capitalism," he cried, bringing his stick to the ground. "Excessive corruption!" he shouted and struck the ground again. "We have all been victims…of extortion, of violence, even of kidnapping for absurd ransom." Abuelo struck his stick with every word, absorbing the room's attention.

Yab shivered when he saw his Abuelo like that. True passion burned within him.

"To top it all off, we're now battling a pandemic. But are we ready to throw in the towel and begin an exodus from our beautiful valley like the Mayans did three thousand years ago?" Abuelo lowered his voice, full of emotion and pain. Then, he dispelled all that with a smile. "How far do you think we elders would make it in those caravans? Would the younger men carry me in their arms all the way up to the border? Or do you fellows think that my walking stick has a motor and a pair of wheels?" Abuelo said and chuckled again, along with the other farmers sharing a laugh, dispelling the initial darkness.

"No, my friends, we cannot let this time of hardship be the collapse of our community. We've been through worse, but guess what? We've prevailed because we're still here, aren't we?

This is just the beginning. No other place in the world has the extraordinary farming heritage or rich lands that we have. Are we willing to turn our heads the other way and ignore this tremendous potential? Are we willing to stop trying and forget about the progress our ancestors achieved throughout the centuries, ruling this entire land we now call our own? I won't deny that we still have lots to sort out; yes, our soil is depleted, and yes, there is less rain and more plagues than before. But, do you know the answer to all that?"

The co-op leaders kept exchanging puzzled gazes with one another every time Abuelo made a brief pause during his speech.

"We have the technology now to overcome all that," Abuelo said. "I'm the eldest here, and even I know that we can use these new technologies to improve our harvest; don't tell me you don't know any better!

A few laughs spread amongst the crowd again.

"The key to growth, employment, and competitiveness is in the land you own. Give thanks to God you have that land! Others have nothing in this world," he said in a serious tone. Abuelo was a very eloquent communicator but could also be a very strict teacher. "Ask yourself what you can do for your land and not what your land can do for your selfish interest, and you'll be surprised by the outcome!

"If we would stop for a second to reflect on our behavioral patterns, I assure you, we would avoid falling into self-sabotaging decisions such as renting our land to tight-fisted mass producers that ruin it by using non-organic fertilizers. Do we even have the right to complain when we're the ones who condone such detrimental practices on our land? Start taking care of it like you take care of your own children; at the end of the day, it supplies their most basic needs. Let's formally begin sustainable practices to counter environmental degradation," he said, speaking to the farmers the same way he spoke to Yab when he was young. "The Mayans left because they didn't know land could be restored."

The farmers seemed a little upset at Abuelo's remarks. They loved him, but Abuelo challenged their worldviews—as he always did—and confronted them directly in a way no one had in quite some time.

"Don't you dare give me that look," Abuelo said, half-jokingly, half-scoldingly. "I know what you are all thinking: 'All of this you proclaim would require plenty of study time, serious work, and collective reformation, but we don't have time for any of that,' or my personal favorite, 'we were not born into a privileged environment to support our goals.' You are wrong if you think like that! If you want to deepen your pockets, as we all want—and there's no shame in that—you have to do things right. You have to improve your skills. There's no easy way to multiply your money or to achieve success. Criminals employ an effortless mindset to wealth without working or struggling, and that's why our country is in such a primitive condition!"

A few of the people in the crowd seemed insulted. The others were somber as Abuelo's words resonated with their way of thinking, grabbing them and rattling their core. Abuelo scanned the crowd thoroughly, studying their faces.

"Juan…yes, you! Stand up," Abuelo said gently, facing one of the farmers. "How much do you rent your land for?"

"Not much, señor," Juan responded. "But I don't have to do any work."

"How many of your grandchildren have left?" Abuelo asked.

"Four, the last one this month," Juan said.

"Juan, you're in your fifties. You're still a young man. Why do you want to sit back and do nothing while you could be exploiting your resources far more efficiently? Don't you want to embrace a new challenge and explore what you can do, Juan?"

Juan thought about it for a moment.

"Your grandchildren could have stayed here, with you, working the same land your grandfathers harvested before your time and prior to teaching you their ways. You could have been doing the same, but your grandchildren left because the money from just renting the farm isn't enough, is it?"

"No, señor." Juan lowered his head, embarrassed.

"This goes for all of you. I know we are stubborn, especially at this age, but I implore you to keep an open mind to the presentation because this young man here"–Abuelo turned and pointed toward Yab–"came up with a solution to many of our problems as a community–problems that are deeply rooted in a collectively endorsed attitude of conformism. I take pride in watching this young man work hard and follow his passion with all his heart, especially when as a result of it, he seeks to see our community thrive. The fact that he's my grandson only makes me more proud."

Abuelo turned with tears in his eyes and looked at Yab in a way Yab had never seen before. There were so many emotions behind those tears–so much passion and reverence. His Abuelo was so proud. He puffed his chest and turned back to the farmers, wiping the tears with the back of his hand.

"My boy followed the caravan toward what they call the American Dream, and thank God, he's back safe now. He left a boy and returned a man, knowledgeable, more hard-working than ever before, and he came back so no one else would have to leave again–to bring the American Dream here to our community," Abuelo said with a trembling voice. "I can assure you that Yab is blessed with the Mayan fire and passion like all of you natives of this land. Besides being a chef, he turned out to be a merchant trader like our ancestors." Abuelo chuckled, and so did the farmers, knowing the legends of the area. "Please, listen to what he has to say, and you won't regret it. We have to trust and empower the younger generations, and I have total trust in Yab's ability to turn this situation around. He came knocking, and I pray that we all answer our doors!"

And with this, despite being told he couldn't be closer to the crowd because of covid, Abuelo walked up to them and began distributing hugs to the people where his heart belonged.

Yab felt so proud of and honored by his Abuelo that he could only wish to have inherited the man's skills as a compassionate motivator and educator because it was clear to Yab that what the farmers needed was education and that it would take lots of time and patience.

Abuelo turned to Yab and hugged him tightly. "You have nothing to worry about," Abuelo said, squeezing Yab in his arms. "I have total faith that you can do this!"

Yab greeted the elder farmers properly once again and stood in the middle, ready to present his arguments. "I believe you all have heard about my project," Yab started. "And I want you to know that I don't seek to alter your working traditions. However, having learned the untapped potential that exists within the Central American farming community, I think it's time we evolve, as a whole, in agreement, all together as one society".

"I don't mean any disrespect to your Abuelo for believing the idea, but what if we don't want to evolve, kid?" one farmer asked, and some of the others nodded in agreement.

"Things are going well for us," another said.

"You're still young!" another said. "You don't know how things work yet. You left for the US and skipped the back-breaking fieldwork; you didn't spend your time working in your father's field like we did and like our sons have already begun to! With what authority do you come and try to shake our foundations?"

"What's wrong with the way we do things?" another added. The murmuring was slowly growing, causing a hubbub.

"There's nothing wrong…for now," Yab said. "That doesn't mean that we should conform, though–or be afraid of change. We need to evolve…to secure a better future for ourselves and the generations to come."

The crowd silenced, waiting for Yab to continue.

"I thought long and hard about the best way to demonstrate what I mean," Yab said. "It wasn't easy, but I think I have the best example."

"Save it, kid. We're tired of utopic statistics being thrown in our faces; we're tired of smartasses and their smokescreens," one farmer said.

Yab did his best to let the comment slide without answering back. "No fake statistics or lies, I promise. I came here to speak from the heart about what I saw and learned in the US," Yab said. "You see, during my time abroad, after the competition, I met with this man's family."

Yab turned and pointed at Phil. "This man invited me for dinner with his lovely family, and that's when I learned more about how young people see the world. That's when a lightbulb blinked in my head. Did you know that there are currently eighty million–yes! eighty million– millennials in the US right now? And there are approximately ninety million Gen Z children, slowly growing, making their own money, spending, becoming a part of the market tapestry!"

The farmers exchanged looks with one another in a mocking fashion, waiting to see where Yab was heading with all of this.

"You see, when I met with these young adults, I realized that we had been looking at things from the wrong angle all this time," Yab said. "And that we haven't been adapting to the evolving consumer needs. All the big corporations around the world do, changing their standards and strategies to meet the demands of the new generations that sprout in the world! Why don't *we*? How long do we expect to keep using the same methods and processes before the big families decide that they can't sell any of our produce anymore?"

The farmers sat in uneasy silence.

"The new generations love plant-based foods, a fact that immediately drives demand for our chili peppers and spices up!" Yab's conviction flowed naturally through his words "Take Phil's son, for example. His name is Alex and he's a millennial, and also one of my first customers in the restaurant I worked for in the US. I grew to know that young man because I adapted to his needs and served him a plant-based dish. Alex occasionally eats meat, following a flexitarian diet because even though he can't abandon meat, he understands the value of reducing meat consumption. Let me also point out that after adapting to Alex's needs, the restaurant grew to be a massive success with younger customers, who progressively started to surge in to try a savory plant-based dish!

"Alex told me about the endless press articles and online documentaries condemning meat and how publishers connect it to the greenhouse effect!" Yab said. "This age group cares about climate change, and they fight not only with their words but with their market choices. They seldom support meat producers anymore; therefore…do you know what that means? They support your community! The whole-food farmers!"

The farmers now leaned forward, listening with great interest.

"Sara, Alex's sister, is Gen Z, and she never eats meat, following a totally vegan diet. I think she visited the restaurant I was working in, right?" Yab made eye contact with Phil, who confirmed Yab's statement with a nod. "You see, these kids aren't like us, with chickens running all over our front yards and cows mowing our lawn for breakfast. They live in the cities, and they actively boycott the big meat retailers. They care about the animals' lives and the disgusting conditions in the livestock industry. Pair that with the carbon emission issue, the pollution, the great cost of the meat industry, and the idolization of the organic solutions...and it's no surprise that more and more Gen Z young adults are turning to vegan and plant-based diets!"

"But busy as we all are, only the two companies authorized to export traditional meat to the US are making money right now, leaving the plant-based market unexplored, creating an opportunity for more and more producers like us to join! The demand for the meat industry won't be around forever, and once the large farmers decide to enter the plant-based market, it might already be too late!"

The farmers started discussing among themselves in agitated whispers. Yab really made a good point.

"So, I kindly ask you all to consider my proposition, which doesn't come out of need or greed, but out of a desire to see our region publicly receive the merit it deserves, to help it succeed globally! The time for us to emerge and stand out is finally here, and we can't ignore it or we'll be run over. We mustn't perish like the Mayans, our ancestors, because they didn't adapt. We need to educate ourselves, myself included, and we need to search for new answers! I have the seeds for you, the knowledge, and the tools thanks to Phil's amazing team and researchers, and if you ask the other farmers that have already joined the Spice Society, you'll know that I am reasonable in my approach, my fixed prices, and consistent in all that I have to offer."

Yab looked at the crowd with eyes full of anticipation and passion, with sheer desire, "Please help me make this something great, for us, our families, and our community! One thing I can promise you is this: I won't sleep until your products are sold to all the Alexes and Saras out there. We are already many steps ahead in the process and I can vouch for that. My partner Phil has ample experience with market distribution structures, and he already cooked up a business plan. All we are waiting for is…you!"

The farmers turned and formed a small circle, whispering to one another as the Cooperative always did. They had to evaluate their presentation and decide if they deemed the idea good enough.

After a few minutes of whispering arguments and talks, the farmers turned to Yab, their eyes serious. It was an important decision after all, and Yab didn't expect them to take it lightly.

"Yab," said Mr. Rodriguez, one of the eldest farmers, "you talk the talk; we'll give you that… But will you walk the walk? We can't say we're impressed, unfortunately. We know where you come from; your father is a good man, and your Abuelo is a man we all respect. Even though we know that your intentions are good, we have families to feed, debts to pay…responsibilities. We can't just put all that on hold."

Mr. Rodriguez was an icon, and many were surprised that he had even shown up since they viewed him as the epitome of tradition. No one expected him to partake in the conversation.

"You make some valid points, but how can we trust you?"

A short silence followed, and the farmers began talking to one another once again. *Mr. Rodriguez made a valid point,* Yab thought.

A short and awkward silence followed. Yab was looking inwardly as he grew nervous, searching for what else to say. *I've explained everything. What else do they want?* Yab was at a loss for words until someone broke the short pause.

"The greater the risk, the greater the reward," Dominic shouted through the silence.

He received a few angry stares and a reproachful scoff from Mr. Rodriguez. That was certainly not the answer they had been waiting for.

"Dominic makes a valid point," Pete, another farmer shouted. "I'm sick and tired of being paid less and less just because we don't live in the city! I like what the boy suggests!"

"No one here is responsible for you having a dozen children, Pete," another farmer said jokingly. "We could give you a fortune and you'd still complain!"

The comment flooded the entire area with laughter coming from almost every one of the attendees, and it was followed by several sarcastic comments from different farmers, and the seriousness of the atmosphere was replaced with jokes and teasing.

"Enough with the jokes!" Mr. Rodriguez shouted, slamming his stick on the ground, coughing violently. "We're here to make an important decision for the future of our children. Save the jokes for later! This is how we always make decisions. Jokes, sarcasm. We have guests in our house, and you still behave that way. Give these men the respect they have earned so far and focus!"

The joyful atmosphere turned cold again. Mr. Rodriguez commanded as much respect as Yab's Abuelo amongst the farmers. The farmers lowered their heads and let Mr. Rodriguez take the lead of the conversation.

"You say that there's an entire market out there, now blooming, correct?" Mr. Rodriguez asked.

"Exactly," Yab said.

"And you want us to be part of your movement, and you promise that we will earn more, adapt our ways, learn to compete with the big corporations now that it's still early," Mr. Rodriguez said again. His tone was brief and commanding. It was a recap of Yab's speech's most important points, stating them in a way as if commanding Yab to commit to his promises.

"That is correct," Yab said. "I *know* that we can compete!"

"And how are you planning to educate these people that for generations have done nothing but work the fields? And I'm speaking for myself here. I'm old, and there are not many tricks you can teach an old dog. What are you going to teach me that I don't already know or that I can learn," Mr. Rodriguez narrowed his eyes.

There wasn't hate or anger behind his stern look but hope that Yab could persuade him. All he needed was an extra push. Yab saw that in his eyes and took hope. If he could persuade Mr. Rodriguez alone, at least half the Coop–if not all of it–would be willing to join Spice Society.

"With all due respect, Mr. Rodríguez, that is the very reason why it's going to be so easy to teach them. All the new production technologies, international good practices, and seed varieties have one thing in common: they all revolve around the fields, something you know very well sir–better than anyone here. It will be easier for you to learn all we have to teach you! Moreover, everything we'll teach them aims to get the best production possible out of the farmers' fields. Isn't that what we all want? Better, smarter work for more efficient management of our people's resources, and thus better pay? Don't all the tools we use aim for the same thing? Only now, we need to reevaluate our tools!" Yab responded confidently.

"I see," Mr. Rodriguez said. "I hope you understand that I have nothing but respect for you, Yab. I just can't take this decision lightly."

"Of course, I understand," Yab said.

"So, all these 'new technologies, methods, and seeds' you've mentioned. Who exactly is going to pay for all that? Last time I checked, we still hadn't figured out how to grow money on trees. And the businessmen I know…they've never been at risk in an operation with the farmers, so I don't think it's your gringo friend who'll carry the burden," Mr. Rodriguez continued, putting Yab in a tough spot.

"Except, we're not like any local business you have ever dealt with in this country, and I'm not trying to be obnoxious, but there are two key factors at play: First, we count on the full support of the impact investment's prize money and a team of expert investors who believe in this project and are willing to bear the necessary expenses to develop this beautiful project! So, for this year and next year's harvest, we'll take care of the new seed and technology expenses. However, since our goal is to make this system sustainable, we'll expect you to bear the costs for the following years, knowing that your profits will grow.

"On the other hand, we're so confident in the success of this new model, that we will also hire a high-end technical team that will work side-by-side with the farmers for a couple of months so that you can all learn everything there is to know. Also, we trust that you will faithfully pass this wisdom to the next generations so that we can keep on growing together."

"I want to believe in you, kid…but we've been let down so many times…and it all sounds too good to be true."

"With all due respect, sir…don't be mistaken. It won't be easy at all! Of course, we're excited, inspired, and motivated, and that's why perhaps we have made it sound so nice and easy; but it will take time, work, sweat, collaboration, and breaking out of many prejudices and blind spots our community has."

At this point, an exaggeratedly high-pitched voice repeated the phrase earlier said by Dominic. "The greater the risk, the greater the return!"

Several angry, frustrated eyes turned toward Dominic, who stood between them, looking left and right for the person who had uttered the phrase.

It was Mr. Rodriguez's young grandson mimicking Dominic, showing natural affection and attraction to Yab's passion in the meeting. The farmers erupted in laughter.

"You don't want to go mimicking this man, kid," a farmer told the young boy.

Mr. Rodriguez couldn't help but quietly chuckle, though he was quick to return the serious look to his face. The rest of the farmers stopped laughing, turning to Mr. Rodriguez, patiently waiting for his verdict. Yab said nothing more, afraid that it could be seen as disrespect toward the old man.

We're so close, Yab thought. *A simple nod would suffice. We're so close to making our dreams come true. So close...* He held his breath until Mr. Rodriguez worked his jaw.

"Well, what are you all looking at! You heard the boy..." Mr. Rodriguez patted his grandson on the shoulder. "We'll give it a shot. But don't get me wrong, and don't think that this is a favor toward you or your Abuelo! It's an opportunity and I would be a damn fool if I turned it down now...but remember, if you mess it up, kid, there won't be no Abuelo that will be able to get you out of this one, I warn you".

"I won't let you down, Mr. Rodriguez; quite the contrary, you will remember this as the best business decision you have ever made, and so will your grandson!" Yab said, confidently.

Yab shook hands with everyone and they invited him and Phil to stay for dinner, enjoying a moment of celebration and the beginning of something hopeful–something new.

Not long after this meeting, even the most stubborn farmers decided to join the Spice Society, forming a formidable family that stood against corruption, micropolitics, and the community's most reprehensible flaw: conformism. They stood united, enjoying each other's help, company, and support, marching together toward a brighter future.

• • •

Phil, Abuelo, and Yab returned to Spice Society's offices, filled with new energy, their faces carved with ecstatic smiles. They were positively restless, eager for the new challenges that awaited them.

"You did it!" Phil exclaimed as they entered Yab's office.

"*We* did it," Yab said.

"This is a very important accomplishment," Abuelo said, full of pride.

"It was thanks to you, Abuelo," Yab said.

"Nonsense," Abuelo responded. "*You* persuaded, Mr. Rodriguez. Even I couldn't have done that. He is a very stubborn man, you know."

Yab felt that he had just conquered one of the biggest obstacles, one of the most complicated milestones in this journey. Even after going through so many challenges, Yab had to keep evolving, always being on his toes, because this was just the beginning.

"Now, now we start meeting with big companies," Phil said with a grand smile. "It won't be easy, but we have achieved so much in such a short period. I think we'll be all right."

"When do we start? I am very anxious, who are we going to offload all of our production to?" Yab asked. "The existing commitment from buyers is very small!"

"Tomorrow," Phil said. "I'll book us a couple of tickets as soon as I get a response from our newest potential client," Phil said, with a bright smile. "I got us a meeting with Millennial Quality Foods. However, I was waiting for us to close the farmer's issue first, before setting a date with them and telling you about it. All we need is a good presentation–as powerful as the one you just delivered to Mr. Rodríguez–so let's get working!" Phil had captivated the multinational giant MQF, he had already been on a few phone calls with the company's CEO and, his personal sensation was that it was now just a matter of polishing final details and signing. Now, landing something of this size would be enough for Yab to guarantee the farmers peace of mind.

A couple of hours had gone by when Phil received confirmation for the meeting for the day after tomorrow. It was perfect for them, as this would enable them to rest and process their victory with the farmer community and work on the client presentation the following day.

They spent that night in Abuelo's house under the stars in the company of the macaws. Yab kept staring at the clear sky he had missed so much, enjoying the view. It all made sense to him now. He had mastered the goals he set, and more goals shined amidst the ocean of options and choices. Yab was ready for what would soon follow.

He had finally convinced the farmer community. He looked back at his grand achievement and considered it one of the most complicated milestones of his journey thus far. But with his goal constantly fired up in his mind, and while constantly trying to make ends meet, his inner warrior always helped him find the greatest solution: he made it through hard work and perseverance. He always thought about his community.

The farmers and his restaurant's customers, and you could tell because he was always on the lookout for the finest flavors. Just for them.

Then, the next day came and they spent the entire day working on the presentation, with Abuelo pitching in with his wise comments from time to time until they had an even better presentation in their hands, feeling confident that no client could resist their offer.

18

A TASTE OF HOME WHEREVER YOU ARE

The plane picked up speed, humming and groaning, and with a gentle push, they left Yab's homeland, like the macaws, cruising through the sky amidst the clouds.

Phil raised his hand and ordered one glass of whiskey for him and a sweet beverage for Yab. The flight attendant brought them their drinks and wished them a pleasant trip. Yab thanked her, even though he wasn't thirsty at all.

"Don't tell me you're still afraid of planes after so many trips" Phil said with a laugh, watching Yab, who was still staring outside the window.

"No, it's not about the trip," Yab said absentmindedly.

"What is it then?"

"The meeting," Yab said. "This really means a lot to me. I want to do it right this time."

"You have nothing to worry about," Phil said. "We went through the supply plan–what–a hundred times? You'll nail it, and you'll always have me as a backup anyway."

"What if they don't like the idea?" Yab asked. "We'll be back at square one. We need a large buyer to sell our product to. The small-time buyers we have lined up won't make the cut forever."

"We'll figure something out," Phil said. "We've got your inner warrior to guide us through, don't we?"

Phil took a sip of his whiskey with an encouraging smile.

Yab looked outside the window as the fluffy patches of white clouds flew beside them, vanishing in the distance. He once had to walk from Copán to the US for weeks, with scarcely more than spare change in his pocket, hoping that he could enter the country even without the proper documentation. Now, the trip would only last for a few hours in the plane's comfort. Phil had vouched for him and secured a business visa. Everything was easier now.

We really have come a long way, Yab thought and felt reassured that if they had made it this far, somehow they would make it even further. Yab squeezed the spinner in his hand. The thought that everything would work out in the end comforted him. God and his Abuelo's manifesting practices were by their side at all times.

As soon as the plane landed, they spotted a flashy digital banner that read "Millennial Quality Foods: *As good as it gets.*" Reading the name of the company they had a meeting with, watching its letters flash by, formed a knot in Yab's stomach. They couldn't lose another minute of time that might be used to rest and prepare.

They hailed a yellow taxi cab that drove them directly to their hotel. Yab was almost proud to see that the hotel wasn't far from his old home, only a couple of kilometers away. Memories washed over him–his arrival in the US and the hardships he had to endure. His old job-hunting now turned to a pitch before a big-time potential client. Yab had grown, and so had his ideas.

During his time in the hotel, Yab was restless. Their meeting had to wait for another three hours, but he kept pacing the floor, practicing his discourse time after time. It had to be perfect. If this deal with Millennial Quality Foods went through, all his dreams would become a reality. The months of work he had put in with Phil preparing for this meeting would feel rightfully compensated. It would be a milestone not only in Yab's career but his life as well–and to the lives of all the farmers trusting him back home.

Calm and composed, Phil managed to grab brunch and even took a quick power nap while Yab kept practicing, taking mental notes of all the ideas he had to share, all the numbers they had prepared. Time went by like a quick, agitated breath, and the meeting was soon about to begin.

A taxi took them from the hotel to the company's headquarters, which were lavish and pristine, clean, smelling of citrus and lavender with a plethora of light surging through the windows, illuminating the variety of plants from the lobby room all the way to the last floor where the meeting would take place.

"Wow, this is a lot," Yab murmured.

"Don't let it go to your head," Phil whispered sarcastically. "It's simply a company, just like Spice Society, but with a hell of a lot more expensive furniture!" Somehow Phil managed to keep a straight face after his joke and reverted to a more serious tone. "You know your worth and The Spice Society's too, so just be yourself and let your words flow."

Yab nodded, though failing to convince himself. What was a small-time cook like him doing with these big-shot executives? Yab shook his head, dismissing the feelings of dread. *No, I have the right to be there,* Yab told himself and held the sun's texture between his fingers. This was an attempt of his internal dialogue to put down his self-image. He wouldn't allow that. He had worked hard and strived his entire life, Yab told himself again, stronger this time, affirming his own values like his parents did all those years. He had as much right to be here as anyone else did.

The elevator doors dinged open, bringing them down an expensive hallway with leather chairs and a carpeted floor. The founder's image greeted them inside, his name inscribed beneath the great portrait.

A man with an expensive outfit and an even flashier smile was waiting for them in the hall. "You must be Yab. I'm Robert, but you can call me Rob," the man said, supplying a firm handshake. "Phil, we spoke on the phone."

"Yab, this is the supply chain manager," Phil explained.

"Pleasure to meet you, Rob," Yab said.

"This way," Rob said. "We've been waiting for you."

The man opened a set of double doors into a conference room with a long table. Mr. Clay himself, the company's CEO, was already sitting behind the conference room's long table.

They exchanged pleasantries quickly, with Mr. Clay asking mundane questions out of courtesy, his eyes scanning Yab and Phil's business plan. He finally set it aside and looked Yab in the eye.

"The floor is yours, and we're all ears."

Phil took a seat on the sidelines as Yab set up the projector with the digital presentation Phil's team had prepared for them.

Yab looked at Clay and Rob, who were staring at him with inquisitive eyes. Yab's hands were shaking, so he reached into his pocket and briefly held the spinner in his hand. Calmness washed over him as the sun, the macaws, the warrior, and the stars shared their protective guidance.

Then, Yab started his presentation. He shared all the points he had raised at the Impact Investment Venture Challenge but in a more efficient way, expanding on his business plan with numbers he managed to collect during his time in Copán. Yab shared his experiences with the farmers, how the Spice Society movements had barely started, and how it was growing faster than even he and Phil had anticipated. More farmers were joining, more hands were working with them, and the quality of the healthy ingredients was radically increasing thanks to the R & D team behind the project.

"So, if we work together, rest assured that we will provide you with only the best products; our fresh and ample spice portfolio along with our plant-based and protein-rich alternatives, all delivered in a timely manner. What's more, we support several social initiatives of high impact: We want to help people preserve and pay respect to their Mayan roots, allowing them to avoid illegal immigration by giving them jobs in their home country, and we finance bilingual education in the poorest regions, all while sharing delicious Mayan flavors with the entire world," Yab said proudly, and added, "so just by working with us you are helping society on a large scale, more than you imagine!" He ended his presentation with a bright smile for everyone present.

Phil shot him an encouraging look, almost ready to applaud, but the company's executives didn't share the same enthusiasm.

"Yab, I'll be frank, if I may," Mr. Clay said, leaning forward with an authoritative frown.

"Please do," Yab said politely.

"Pardon me, but I don't see a fit."

The words fell like a pile of bricks on top of Yab. A cold sentiment surged through him, clenching his stomach, just like the few seconds before the plane's takeoff.

"Even though it's got potential, it's too idealistic and a bit romantic; the problem is that we're not angel investors or venture capitalists. We're a renowned multinational, and we like to work with stable, trustworthy business collaborators that have a good and solid track record," Clay said. "We can't put the company's future at stake just because we might like your idea or even believe in it. I don't think your proposal aligns with what we're looking for."

Phil kicked himself up and joined Yab before the prospect's table.

"Idealistic and romantic would mean that we don't have a business plan to support it," Phil interjected.

"Phil…Don't take this the wrong way. I don't mean to offend you– or to undermine the work you have going on here," Clay said bluntly, "But we don't see it; it's as simple as that. We work with many other renowned and internationally certified growers, and everything has been going well so far. We simply don't feel the need to make such a sudden change from that and start buying from an inexperienced supplier like Spice Society. Pursuing a noble cause doesn't make your *service* any better. When we saw your supply projections on paper, we were convinced that your company had been around your country's national market for at least a couple of decades. But now, after hearing you out, we understand that most of these optimistic claims you have made come from the enthusiastic rush you still feel from getting so many farmers on board with your idea. Also, it seems to me that you don't even have a customer base in your home region. You're basically a start-up."

"But we have clear objectives," Yab argued. "We want to create more opportunities for these people, and we want to offer true, authentic foods and spices, which will eventually generate a great amount of profit. All we need is a well-established buyer–someone like you–who is willing to buy the lion's share of our product. After receiving it, all you need to do is add your brand to it and you know that it will sell in no time; it's a great opportunity for you to outgrow your current sales with even higher quality ingredients."

"This all sounds really nice, but this is business, gentlemen. We need partners that we can trust, and based on your short experience, we don't have that trust in you," Rob blurted.

Clay gestured at Rob, asking him to be polite. "What my partner means is that you still lack credibility. As I said, there's potential, but take this as a word of advice: before coming to big corporations or multinationals, you should make a name for yourselves in smaller markets. Get endorsements first; then, go hunting after the big fish. So, to save us all time, I think we should end this meeting right here, but please don't take this as a definite rejection; just follow the process and come back in a few years when you've already seen success with this plan of yours. Then we'll talk. Thank you for your time and for your presentation, but I think we're done for now."

Yab and Phil exchanged a defeated look, dragging their feet out of the conference room, walking back to the hotel to pick up their things and move to a cheaper hotel for the rest of the week.

Night fell, and Yab was sitting by the window, alone, staring at the spinner, thinking about all the people back in Copán, waiting for him to succeed. *Now what?* Yab thought.

Was this the end of Spice Society? Was this the end for Yab and his wild dreams? Without a big consistent buyer in the US, they really couldn't do much with all they had gathered to make. They didn't really have any other alternatives besides Millenium Quality Foods, and if they didn't do something quickly, farmers were going to start losing faith in what was promised to them. Yab imagined Constantino and Mr. Rodriguez's frowning in his mind.

He heard Don Constantino's voice in his head, bitter and full of sorrow. Then, he saw Mr. Rodriguez's face with eyes screaming "I told you so" while waving his finger. How could Yab look them in the eye again after failing this meeting? How could he return and share the bad news? They trusted him with their legacies, and he couldn't deliver what he had promised.

Phil suggested looking for other options, to see if they could salvage something valuable from this trip. Were there any alternatives left? Yab couldn't think of any. He felt naive and inexperienced to have let all of his plans depend on these few meetings with the big corporations. Maybe he had to abandon Spice Society and return to his small restaurant. He comforted himself with the thought that the farmers weren't really into the idea anyway. It would be a fresh reset; he'd just have to forget about impacting the world, about helping the farmers in Copán, and revolutionizing everybody's kitchen. But most importantly, he'd have to forget that he had the potential to achieve all of this.

Yab decided to do what he did whenever he felt battered and beaten down. He pulled out the spinner and gave it a quick whirl. He asked the sun to guard his subconscious, reciting his mantra, but it felt pointless this time. The words didn't feel as strong as they used to.

They felt weak, like a tale he kept repeating to himself to feel good. Yab trusted Abuelo's wisdom. The spinner could work, but…maybe it just wasn't destined for everyone. Yab was fighting an inner battle: on one side there was the unappeasable fighter, sternly holding his ground; on the other, there was the tired young boy who felt he had already done so much and that there was little to nothing else that he could do.

Yab clenched the spinner in his hand, tears running down his cheeks. He had to be strong. He had to persevere as he had for all this time. But he was tired. So tired of enduring all the challenges and the failed attempts. Had he been a fool to believe in all this in the first place?

Wanting to clear his head from all the pain and negative energy, wanting to let the sun coat him in comfort and peace, Yab left the hotel and decided to visit the one place that always calmed him.

In the middle of the night, Yab wandered through the calm summer streets, enjoying the city he'd grown to love these past five years. The smell of the local barbeque blended with the tree's fragrances and created a compelling distraction–one of passion, love, and nostalgia.

Strolling about the fading city, Yab followed his instinct to the place where he felt closest to home: Victor's kitchen.

He could see from afar that the lights were still on, and as he got closer, Yab could hear the loud hubbub of the customers from outside. He pushed the door open, expecting to find a dimming restaurant, close to the last call. To Yab's immense surprise, the restaurant looked more like a market than a diner: it was packed, with more tables than Yab remembered, and all the seats were taken. A host stood at the front, trying to manage the line–more than a dozen people waiting to be served. The host turned to Yab and asked, "Do you have a reservation?"

Yab couldn't answer right away. He was still in awe, watching the restaurant packed with more people than he would serve in a month when he started out–people talking, laughing, and discussing the food excitedly. Yab felt like he was in a dream, experiencing an ideal restaurant. What more could be asked for?

"I told you this place was good," Yab heard a woman say.

"The taste of the sauce is as good as they say," another man added.

"Sir, do you have a reservation?" the host asked again.

"Uh, no, I'm here to see Mr. Victor," Yab said.

The host eyed him carefully.

"Who should I say is asking for him?" the host asked, clicking a pen.

"No way!" Victor exclaimed as he was walking to the foyer of the restaurant, and the entire restaurant came to a serene, anxious halt. "It's Yab! I can't believe my eyes!"

The guests were now looking at him. The host took a step away since his services would no longer be required.

"Everyone, your attention, please," Victor called out, drawing the customers' attention. "This is the man behind the plant-based chicken burger you all enjoy and the sauce and flavors you keep asking about! The genius behind this work of culinary art!" Yab was caught off guard by these statements, but they were heavy enough to make him forget about his problems—at least for a moment—as the customers looked at him with appreciation.

Victor hugged Yab tightly. "Without him, the culinary world would have been worse off!" Victor added.

A few of the customers applauded and others commended his sauce and chicken burger recipe.

"What brings you here, my old friend?" Victor asked.

Yab's frown returned.

They walked to the kitchen and Yab explained everything that had happened ever since he came back to the US, while he observed the completely reformed kitchen.

Victor looked down and responded with a deep sigh, "I'm sorry things didn't go as you expected, but needless to say, there will always be a place for you in this kitchen!"

Yab obviously wasn't relieved by his comment, but Victor pressed on.

"Consider this as well, my friend: I have *never* bought from Millennial Quality Foods! Isn't that right, Jose?"

Yab turned and saw the cook Victor had hired when Yab had to leave.

"Yes, that's right sir! Not once" Jose said.

"And don't get me started on Yab's Mayan Sauce, and on all of the menu's platters; it's all a huge hit!" Victor said. "Just look around! Had I ever imagined the restaurant so full, I would've taken that mortgage and bought that lake house my ex-wife dreamed of…Oh well. But yes, son, the burger is good, but the sauces and spices—darn it…they're on another level!"

"People keep asking me for the "Pollo Chuco's" recipe," Jose chuckled. "Some of them even want to pay me to cook for them at birthdays and other celebrations," José added.

"Hold on," Yab said with a confused look. "Yab's Mayan Sauce?" he said out loud, deeply puzzled.

"Yes! It's your classic sauce–the one you came up with back in the day. I wrote down the recipe and named it after you in your honor, I hope you don't mind," Victor said, "it gives the product a mystical touch, you know what I mean? And people love it, so what's there to change?"

Yab's mind was like the Mayan spinner, all the elements at play, manifesting, generating more and more creative power. He forgot all about his recent meeting, throwing away and suppressing the idea of failure and rejection. The warrior took control, guiding Yab's creative mind toward a solution that had always been there before him.

Phil stormed into the restaurant. He was agitated from all the walking and searching. "Is Yab here?" he demanded, his voice interrupting Yab's thoughts.

Yab turned to Phil enthusiastically, with his eyes wide open.

"Yab, is everything okay?" Phil asked.

"More than okay," Yab said. "Everything is perfect!"

"W-what happened?" Phil asked.

"I know how we can keep Spice Society going," Yab said.

"I'm all ears," Phil said, grabbing a chair.

"Phil," Yab said, trembling, struggling to keep his excitement in check. "I think Victor might have just solved our problem! I think I have a way for us to pivot our business into something greater!"

"What do you have in mind?" Phil asked.

"We need the perfect business model, correct?" Yab asked.

"Let's think outside the box: what if we could get the clients to come looking for us and not the other way around…and grow our brand while we were at it?" Yab asked.

"And how exactly are we going to do that?" Phil asked.

"That's what Victor helped me understand!" Yab said. So many things came to mind, so bear with me, all right? For starters, we could serve our sauces, plant-based ingredients, and spices through restaurant dishes that customers already enjoy!

"Phil's face was a complete puzzle."

Yab continued, "our direct clients in this scenario would be the restaurants." We cater to them with our entire product portfolio and we can start by asking Victor to let us mention our brand in his menu in exchange. That way, whenever a person orders the BBQ chicken wings at Victor's, a criollo chicken basket, or even a plant-based chicken, they will know it's all made with our seasoners, our sauces, our breader mixes, and our plant-based solutions. This leads me to the second part of the plan; call it a 'strategic shortcut' to the tracking record issue that Clay brought up. Since our quality would be made known through people's restaurants of choice, we could then start selling retail products to the customers in a small area of each restaurant– maybe the front desk? I'm sure that Victor wouldn't mind if we bottle our products and sell them at the cash register as a test…

"Two birds, one stone; if we pull this off…we could move on to a whole new level of business!"

"It would be my pleasure, Yab. It's done already!" Victor pleasantly exclaimed.

Phil was puzzled. "What are you saying, Yab," Phil exclaimed. "How exactly does this solve our problems?"

"You see, Phil, we don't necessarily have to sell our products to the big corporations since we can find thousands of restaurants like Victor's out there–restaurants that will buy our products in bulk–and simultaneously, their customers will get to know our brand, so we can later bottle up our products and sell directly to them. Plus, we already have

Victor's restaurant as a success reference, which proves for a fact that our products have been a hit!"

"Please elaborate," Phil asked kindly, as he started to understand the idea.

Yab was happy to explain. "Victor, do you still keep the spices on the top shelf?"

Jose answered him first. "No! Yab, we keep them on the lower shelf, or else I wouldn't be able to reach so high to get them," he said laughing.

Yab took out one of his classic easy-to-apply cassava breader mixes and showed it to Phil. Then, he asked Victor to get him a bottle of Yab's Mayan Sauce, and he placed both of them flat on a silver table in the middle of the kitchen.

Yab turned to Jose. "Jose, please get a customer to come to the kitchen. Tell them they won a quick tour, or make something up, but just bring them back here!"

Jose quickly complied and brought a couple, both loyal guests who visited the restaurant every week.

Yab greeted them enthusiastically with a smile.

"I would like to ask you a question and please be honest," Yab said, holding the cassava breader mix in one hand and the sauce in the other, both lids open. "Okay, smell these."

The couple took a good sniff.

"Okay, now, can you tell which of the platters we use these ingredients in?" Yab asked.

"Of course," the woman said, pointing at the breader mix. "This is what Jose uses in the plant-based chicken sandwich."

"What about this one?" Yab asked, wiggling the sauce in his hand.

"I'll answer that," the husband said with pride. "That's the sauce that comes with most of the options here. Or I should say, my greatest addiction." He laughed, unashamed.

"How do you know that these products are good?" Yab asked.

The couple exchanged a puzzled gaze, wondering if there was a trick to the question.

"Be honest," Yab insisted. "There's no wrong answer."

"Well," the husband said. "I have grown to trust Victor very much, and I love the chicken burger, so I've come to eat here every Sunday for the last year. Every time I say that we should eat out less, the sauce keeps bringing me back!"

"Okay, Yab said. "And if Victor were to sell the sauce and the breader as stand-alone retail items, would you buy them?"

The man's eyes widened. "Would I buy them? I would bring a shopping cart with me every time I came over to the restaurant! I would love to use it at home when cooking for my family!"

Yab thanked the happy couple and handed them the sauce and the breader mix as a gift.

"Can we really keep them?" the woman asked in disbelief.

"Of course, you earned them!" Yab said.

The husband's eyes lit up with enthusiasm, "I hope you decide to sell this sauce one day."

The couple left, discussing with excitement, leaving the rest back in the kitchen alone once again.

"You see, Phil, this couple we just interviewed…they know they love our product despite the fact that we haven't been around in the market for decades as Clay demanded; and not only that, but they also seem to prefer us over their traditional alternatives."

Yab continued, "they know that our product is exquisite because they walked into this restaurant and tried it. But here comes the key:

They didn't have to stop and think to choose our brand over any other, because it was literally what was served on their plate–and you heard it yourself, they would buy it for their loved ones too because it's *that* good.

"Which means that we've found the solution to our "track record" issue; all we have to do is start channeling our product directly through restaurant chains; we can sell directly to restaurants, and if things go well, maybe someday we can even sell our products to nearby supermarkets and retail stores–even sell on the internet, who knows!

"What better way to promote the sauce than through restaurants, serving it along with good homemade food and allow our immigrants to have a tase of home wherever they are?" Yab said. "We could start knocking on other chicken restaurant's doors and start selling them our cooking system, using Victor's restaurant as a reference success case, if he agrees, of course!

"So, these restaurants would buy our menu?" Phil asked. "What would you sell them exactly?"

"That's only part of what we'd be doing. What you're referring to–selling a menu–is called food service."

"Okaaay," Phil said in a confused tone, inviting Yab to continue his explanation.

"Let me explain: In the food service, as part of our plan, we would most likely have to personally visit different restaurant entrepreneurs to offer them our know-how, including menu creation, recipes, ingredients, and specific machines and cooking techniques that cooks should use if they wish to obtain the tastiest chicken ever, and they would also be able to count on us for technical support whenever they need to."

The reason I want to do this, Phil, is to help restaurant owners design menus with better quality and variety; after all, remember that many of them are untrained immigrants, not chefs.

"Most importantly, we'll help Central American cooks solve a great problem that they're facing with the preparation of their ethnic foods here in the US…They're forced to use local substitute ingredients instead of the original ones–those of Central American origin–and this is because their current Central American food suppliers do it this way in order to cut down export expenses; hence cooks have lost the real taste and thus their menu's authenticity. We'll bring real, colorful flavors from Mayan lands to their Kitchens to restore the authentic flavors. Customers will love it! Just wait and see. They'll feel like they're back home, and locals will be introduced to exquisite new flavors!"

"Good, Yab! This is a very innovative way of promoting our own products–through foods people already enjoy!" Phil said. "Restaurant owners implement our formulas, our recipes, and ingredients and display our brand name in their menus, sort of like the "intel inside" logo on computers of different brands, right They would also sell our retail food products up front, close to their cashiers, which would be like a cherry on the cake."

Phil's excitement slowly turned into a mild frown, and Yab immediately worried.

"What's wrong?"

"Well," said Phil, "all of this makes sense, but I'm worried about the time it will take for us to sell the entire production we've already bought and secured in Central America since this will determine how fast we'll be able to pay the farmers and the rest of suppliers–not to mention paying off the bank loan."

"Yes, Phil, I already thought about that, and as much as it hurts to say it, I think Clay was right with his piece of advice. I see no other way to grow than to expand our sales in our neck of the woods before going international. We need to launch in Central America and establish the foundational pillars of our business there and the guarantee of our authenticity.

All of a sudden, Phil smiled! There was something on his mind–an idea bigger than Yab had expected, just like always.

"Speak already!" Yab said frantically.

"You were the one talking about thinking outside the box," Phil finally said. "Since we're going to launch big in Central America, why don't we take it a step further? What if we target the food industry as a whole? After making a name for ourselves among chicken restaurant owners and entrepreneurs, we can start offering our very own spice mixes, not only to the chicken restaurant industry but also to different food manufacturers: from fried chip companies to frozen foods to whoever else wants to buy our spectacularly engineered spice mixes and add them to their retail products...everybody wins!"

It took a second for Yab to take it all in and digest it. "Lots of work ahead of us, Phil..."

Phil continued, "We'll offer big and small food brands the alternative of buying spices prepared by us: Yab's classical breader mix, the tropical herbs and pepper batch, our garlic and parsley sauce mix, the orange-bbq sauce, and so many more! Think about it," he said excitedly, "at some point we might even manage to have mainstream customers try it–and even like it–which would make the market size all the more interesting for us to sell this flavor of yours!"

Jose, Victor, Phil, and Yab looked at each other with enthusiastic smiles, as they all felt that something great was emerging. They were all waiting for Yab's reaction; all eyes were pointing at him. "You had me from the start," Yab exclaimed. "Let's get to work!"

19

A PLATFORM THAT ELIMINATES SYSTEMIC POVERTY

Yab stood at the open window's edge, staring at the street where everything began, taking a long breath of the city's familiar smell.

A soft knock came on the door. Yab crossed the old apartment he used to rent, and he now owned. It was his second base of operations in the US, an apartment he grew to love and cherish. He had redecorated, fixed the radiators, and added a homely air of Copán to it. It was one of the first things he bought, a symbol of his life in the US, a place he never wanted to part ways with.

Yab had been spending a lot of time on the road, traveling from Copán to the US and back, getting involved in every aspect of his business, from production to delivery, and now with the restaurants coming, Yab had to travel around all the time. It was nice to have a base of operations in the US, though. The neighborhood used to be shady, but lately, with more immigrants from around the world formalizing their new home and more stores opening, the neighborhood came to life, vibrant and inviting. A true melting pot. It reminded Yab of home, and he couldn't pass on the opportunity of taking the apartment.

Yab opened the door and laid eyes on Phil, who was well dressed, flashing his vibrant smile.

"Ready to go?" Phil asked. "Lots to do in Copán."

"Give me just one second," Yab said and turned back inside the house, moving to the old desk that he refused to change.

His fingers slid across the surface. He could still feel the marks he had carved, one for each failed attempt, and one for each successful one. Yab opened the top drawer and took a wooden chest out, placing it on the desk.

He blew the dust off the surface and wiped the rest with his palm. The chest screeched open, revealing the one treasure Yab hadn't touched for years.

It's been so long, my friend, Yab thought, grabbing the old spinner in his hand, feeling the textures once again.

His smile widened. It was as if the textures and the symbols were now engraved with Yab's history. A simple touch took him to the beginning of it all–to the struggles, the challenges, and eventually the success.

I think it's time for you to return home, Yab thought and squeezed it with nostalgia, remembering all the times the spinner had helped him overcome the challenges in his life.

"I'm ready," Yab told Phil. "Let's go!"

Yab and Phil packed their bags and went back to Central America since they had to get the whole operation going if they wanted to achieve all they had planned for. Yab's time flew by, as he was either on the move to get new clients or figuring out production, quality control, R&D, and the supply chain. Similarly for Phil, with his myriad investments in other companies, life passed by, meeting after meeting. And this went on for both of them for the following five years.

The Spice Society quickly grew and became a family of approximately four hundred employees and over a thousand farmers in just that short time selling in Central America, which came as a complete surprise to Yab and Phil, but they felt so overwhelmingly blessed by all that was going on that they couldn't think of a better way to react than work harder in order to make the success sustainable. Hard work was also key to fulfilling Yab's ultimate purpose, which he repeated internally every time he remembered:

"Through the creation of business platforms such as Spice Society, together, we'll bridge the gaps between producers, buyers, and consumers around the world, to create abundance for many..."

Yab couldn't believe it, all that he had accomplished–with everyone else's help, of course. He had managed to build a community that was bringing work and education to the underrepresented; but the unbelievable part was his achieving this all whilst practicing his personal passion: serving the tastiest, most flavorful Central American platters to thousands of happy customers.

Just as planned, customers eventually started to wonder how they could take Yab's flavors home, as they kept returning for more to the many different restaurants that Spice Society was selling to.

Therefore, Yab finally made the move and, slowly and strategically, started asking his clients if he could put up small "Mayan marketplaces" within a small space of each restaurant, where he would sell the products directly to the restaurant's customers.

As Spice Society's retail products began to boom, the company started selling in retail stores and supermarkets so that anyone who desired could access Yab's myriad of Latin flavors whenever they wanted.

The Spice Society thrived. Demand was so intense that the platform had to expand, recruiting more families…which was the entire purpose, to begin with!

There was one product in particular that became a star-seller, which was of no surprise to Yab or Phil; but it filled Yab with a great deal of emotion and appreciation for his own professional roots and made him look back at the harsh times all the more gratefully.

Just like the couple at Victor's restaurant once dreamed of, they could now take Yab's Mayan Sauce back home.

"You could come and have a meal every once in a while like you used to, you know?" is what Victor said jokingly to the husband, who was a fanatic, each time he came in to buy a bottle.

It was funny to watch because as soon as the husband walked into the restaurant, almost as if programmed, Jose would take a bottle of "Yab's Mayan Sauce" and place it on the counter.

With the ups and downs of the business world, Yab was managing to keep things afloat, both on a personal and professional level, and time went by and Spice Society kept growing and growing.

By now, it had been seven years since their meeting with Millennial Quality Foods, and not a single day passed by that Yab didn't remember his ultimate purpose of selling internationally, to further scale his goal of creating abundance for many and making a legacy out of his sustainable community.

He now had certifications in place, a track record of several years, and thousands of retail customers, restaurants, and large industrial clients. What would Clay have to say now? At this point, the Spice Society's overall structure and financial position made it much more prepared to take on a giant such as the US. A market with sixty million Latin Americans–a culture of people deeply rooted in their gastronomic customs and traditions. Therefore, the whole lot of them were potential customers, seeking authenticity in their foods, and that wasn't to mention the healthy-eating vegans and flexitarians, the perfect target for Yab's plant-based expertise, which he'd been perfecting in Copán. By this point, he'd obtained a position of leadership in the sector through research, development, and creating unique blends.

20

THE CEIBA TREE

Yab was standing in the middle of his relaunched old restaurant back in Copán, where everything started, now packed with people smiling and nodding at him after every hungry bite.

"You did great with the reopening of our original restaurant, Manuel," Yab said, patting his old friend on the back.

"Thank you, Don Yab," Manuel said. "It's your recipes that draw the people in, though."

"It takes a skilled chef to recreate even the simplest of recipes," Yab said with a bright smile. "I'm glad we opened this beautiful place again, especially to make our original customers happy."

"It's been my pleasure, Don Yab," Manuel said with excitement.

"Please, just call me Yab," said Yab, flashing a brilliant smile. "Without the Don; we're business partners now. You're the only person I trust to lead this place. You know that this restaurant is dear to my heart: the first, the original Yab's Chicken and Mayan Corner!"

"Thank you…Yab," Manuel said, returning a confident smile.

Just then, Yab's phone rang, interrupting their conversation. "Sorry, I have to take this."

"Don Yab," Emy, his new assistant said. "Mr. Phil wants to confirm your meeting with one of the firm's investors to present Spice Society to him.

"Tell him I'll be there," Yab said.

"Will do, Don Yab," Emy said.

"Thank you, Emy. I don't know what I'd do without you," Yab said and hung up, turning to Manuel.

"Manuel, I have to go now. It's always a pleasure. Promise me you'll teach me the mushroom meat alternative you came up with soon, Manuel," said Yab with a wink.

"Ah, it's not *that* good sir," Manuel argued.

"He's being modest," a customer said from a nearby table, overhearing the conversation. "I'm here every day for those delicious mushrooms!"

"I know he is," Yab said.

Flustered, Manuel averted his gaze from the two men.

"One more thing," Yab said, pulling Manuel closer. "You're not having any problems with the local gangs, are you? If you do, you'll let me know, right?"

"No, no problems so far. Everyone's either working in the fields or are afraid of the people's backlash. We're doing fine."

"I'm proud of you, Manuel," Yab said with one last pat on the shoulder. "I'll be back in a few days."

"Oh, one last question," Yab said. "Does your father still work in your family's souvenir shop?"

"Yeah, why?"

"Nothing," Yab said. "I might need something from him."

Yab exited the restaurant, back to the beautiful cobbled street he'd grown to love. This restaurant felt as much his home as Victor's Restaurant in the US. So many memories filled this street–the good and the bad. They were all part of his life's rich tapestry, all adding up to the man he'd become.

His franchise chicken restaurants and even cloud restaurants that served the food apps were booming, and he was discussing with Phil whether or not to open a few more. Also, a few colleagues had taken interest and bought Yab's menu system to sell at their own restaurants; now, his chicken-traditional and plant-based chicken were being served to thousands of people, and the growers back in Mayan Lands were harvesting more peppers, spices, and plant-based proteins than ever.

The platform he had built now employed thousands of people, most of them in Central America and some others in the US. Therefore, he felt more responsible than ever to take care of this ecosystem. Yab had achieved goals he would've never dreamed possible just a few years prior. He was passionate about his job, and he wouldn't rest until the day he decided to retire. Until then, his life would keep on focusing on becoming better, improving his brand, and providing his best food and sauces to as many people as possible around the world. This was the lifestyle he had adopted with the purpose of making the platform live on throughout the ages.

Yab got in his car and started the engine. He checked the passenger's seat looking for his computer, only to realize that he had forgotten it the night before at the office. His presentation was on it, along with some additional data they had managed to collect and wanted to show to the investor. Shaking his head with a smile of disbelief, Yab drove toward the warehouse on the outskirts of the town.

Putting some Ranchera songs on the radio, Yab turned onto the highway, speeding up through the lavishly green lands that coated everything around him. With the windows lowered, Yab let the dry wind caress his hair and took a deep breath, enjoying every moment of his stay in Copán. In a few days, he would have to leave again. He had to make the most of his stay there, to absorb as much of the energy possible before traveling abroad. He loved this place.

Suddenly, the music stopped and the radio DJ's somber voice filled Yab's car. "We interrupt our program for a very important announcement…"

Yab rolled up the windows and increased the volume, listening carefully.

"Another uproar had started on the highway, slowly moving toward the city with hundreds of infuriated citizens protesting new taxes due to the recent changes in government. The rally is obstructing passage to all citizens and especially political officials."

As the speaker kept talking in the background, Yab's attention turned to the road and noted a roadblock in the distance. At least he was already just a couple hundred meters away from the warehouse. Hundreds of people had banded together, marching slowly toward the city. Fire raging…road flares painting the red twilight sky…hundreds of banners and signs being waved by the crowd…the chanting of people… forcing the entire street to rattle.

Yab stopped the car abruptly before the roadblock and parked it on the side of the road, watching the hundreds of fuming people rally in an unruly line of anger and disgust.

Yab's phone rang shortly after the radio producer had broadcasted the news. It was Phil, who had already been informed about the mess by the warehouse supervisor since the crowd had just passed by right in front of the building.

"Yab, are you alright? Did you hear what's happening?" Phil asked anxiously.

"I'm looking at it right now," Yab said with exhaustion in his voice.

Political instability, once again, Yab thought. It was by far one of his least favorite challenges. A part of Yab only wished he could be one of those men who left their home country and never looked back, not caring about what happened. He wasn't like that, though. He cared, and he cared deeply, as did all of those people protesting the corrupt institutions. His gift was to promote the Mayan lands, to reduce inequality, and to serve as a bridge between his home country and international markets.

"I knew I should carry you with me today," said Yab, shoving his hand in his pocket and clenching the spinner.

Yab looked around. The mob kept marching before him. It would be impossible to get to the warehouse in his car, not with the roadblocks and the hundreds of people before him.

"Phil, are you still there?" Yab asked.

"Yes, what's going on?" Phil asked, still anxious.

"I'm close to the office but I can't get through here," Yab said. "Can you please postpone the meeting? Thirty minutes tops?"

"I'll try to stall him. Don't worry. Just be safe, all right?" Phil said.

"Yes, yes, I will. Don't worry about me. Give me thirty minutes. I'll be there."

Phil and Yab hung up, and Yab turned his attention to the roadblock before him. *What should I do,* Yab thought. As always in situations like this, Yab gave the spinner a try, letting its colors blend.

Instinctively, he stepped out of the car to breathe properly and have time to think. The mob chanted and yelled. The clamor of the march covered everything around them, including Yab's thoughts. Yab had to think. He couldn't come up with a solution with all of this commotion still echoing through the valley.

He locked the car and took a few steps away from the roadblock, onto the crisp grass, still fiddling the spinner in his hand.

As soon as he raised his gaze, Yab saw before him the sprawled branches, hanging right above the street: thick and dense, with their cool foliage covering the better part of the road's side. *Branches represent being best in class at something!* he thought. Yab smiled. It was a tree he knew all too well.

Deep behind the luxuriate foliage spreading over the road, Yab noticed a place he had forgotten for quite some time: The ceiba tree; the same tree, seven years ago, where he first met the caravan of immigrants with whom he took the arduous trip to the US. The same tree his father has spoken of right before he decided to embark on his journey to the US.

The tree was even bigger than Yab remembered. Its branches spread over the road's side and cast their thick shade all about, while its trunk was quite far from the road, inside a friend's lot. As if drawn by magic, Yab walked toward the trunk, leaped over the fence, and witnessed the tree's beauty from up close for the first time.

He reached out and touched the trunk, repeating in his mind, *Honest work through discipline,* feeling its gnarly and uneven texture. Yab closed his eyes, letting his sense of touch absorb the tree's shape, and his smell to become captivated by the beautiful, earthly aromas.

"We haven't seen each other for a while," Yab said. "But you're as stunning as ever."

The uproar grew as the mob progressed, gradually making room for Yab to pass to the warehouse if he so desired.

"You're still here, proud and strong…as is the political instability, inequality, and lack of opportunities of this place," Yab muttered. "This country will never change, will it, old friend? You know, that was the reason I fled in the first place, maybe political conflict, too, is what made the Mayans flee from Copán. Who knows? But I'm here now, and I want to make a difference; I think I've come up with a solution–a pact that can piece things together in my industry. It's a new idea, but I think it might just work."

Yab took a look at his watch. Only five minutes left for the meeting. While the mob had cleared the road, Yab would never make it on time. It didn't matter. After becoming inspired by the tree's presence, he already knew the best way to succeed in this meeting.

"Awesome," Yab said while contemplating the tree and the spinner, which he returned to his pocket.

It was now quiet here, under the tree's trunk, and the Copán Ruins added a historical touch to the background behind him along with the green-gleaming mountains and his Abuelo's home in the distance. *It'd be a unique place to have the meeting if I could get a good connection,* Yab thought.

However, Yab would not be alone in this meeting. He placed his phone on one of the huge roots and remained standing. *Come on, ceiba tree, bless my meeting,* he thought,, then called his most supportive colleagues for help to feature Spice Society and, of course, make him look great! He would need the best, most honest members of the Spice Society.

Yab video conferenced Mr. Rodriguez's son, Pedro, who represented the farmers; Gustavo from the processing plant; Mr. Victor to vouch for the success of his sauce and Yab's work ethic in the restaurant; Carlos, one of the partners in one of his restaurants; and finally Clarisa, a supermarket owner and customer in Jersey, who Yab met a few years ago and still maintained a good relationship with.

"Hello guys," Yab said with a warm smile, greeting his loyal friends and team members.

They greeted him one by one, sharing equally warm, virtual smiles.

"I really appreciate you taking my call, and though you don't know each other," Yab started, "you're all very special members of the

Spice Society and provide tremendous value to our platform–each of you in a different way."

Yab took a few moments to explain the Spice Society platform and how it connected growers with consumers in the US. He had a few more minutes on the clock before the meeting, so he took the time to properly introduce everyone and make them feel comfortable. They all seemed pleased to meet each other for the first time. There was a sense of grandeur, that something bigger than themselves was connecting them, and they could all feel it.

"Why did you call us, Yab?" Pedro asked.

"I'm sorry for the impromptu meeting, but this is an emergency. I really need your help, guys," Yab said.

"Anything you need," Gustavo said.

"Same here," Mr. Victor added.

"Phil and I are presenting Spice Society to an existing investor. However, I cannot get to my computer on time, where I had my presentation, so a better idea occurred to me: I want you guys to be a part of the meeting," Yab said. "You, yourselves, are truly the platform that helps reduce systemic poverty, and I want the investor to see this…if you're willing to help?"

"With pleasure," Clarisa said.

"What do we have to do?" Mr. Victor asked. "I don't know much about the bigger picture."

"Don't worry about a thing," Yab said. "I'll ask each one of you a question and you can respond truthfully and honestly. Are you in?"

"Of course!" Pedro and Gustavo said.

"Sure thing, kid!" Mr. Victor said.

"Okay. Get ready. We're about to join them," Yab said.

Yab logged in Phil, who was already talking to the investor. Yab's bright smile greeted them, dispelling Phil's initial fear.

"Good morning, Mr. Howard. Unfortunately, I couldn't get back to the office on time," Yab started, quickly taking charge of the meeting. "But I hope the scenery behind me will only add to what we have to say."

"Not a problem with me," Mr. Howard said. "If anything, it only shows dedication, considering the sudden turn of events near the warehouse. Phil explained. I'm so sorry!"

"Since you mention it…I had a different presentation in mind, but the recent events inspired me to change its direction," Yab started. "As Phil informed you, there is once again, political instability down here, in these precious but troubled Mayan lands. The riot prevented me from getting back to our offices."

Yab turned the phone toward the mob, slowly vanishing in the distance.

"So, I've decided to invite other dear members of Spice Society to this video meeting," Yab said and introduced everyone by name. "They are the Spice Society. The incredible people you see here today are the heart and soul of Spice Society–the platform that eliminates systemic poverty–and I wanted you to see that for yourself, something we would've missed out on if it weren't for the riot, eh?" Smiling, Yab continued. "I guess everything happens for a reason. "

"It's an honor to meet you," Mr. Howard said.

"And you, Mr. Howard," said Yab. "As I mentioned before, I planned to lead with a different angle, but I want to start by addressing the political instability, something I assume would worry any investor, correct?"

"Truth is, I'm still quite worried about the situation there," Mr. Howard said. "You see, such events and such instability could be of great danger to us in the long run. We're going to take everything with a grain of salt, so to speak."

"I totally understand and respect that, Mr. Howard," Yab said. "That's why I wanted to assure you that in Spice Society, we've been anticipating such instability and we've managed to make risk management part of our contingency plans."

Mr. Howard was skeptical, though somewhat relieved.

"Say, Yab, how do you plan to mitigate such risk?" Mr. Howard asked.

"Very good question, sir," Yab said. "But instead of me answering this question, I want our guests to do it for you. You see, if I made all sorts of grand promises, but these good people here couldn't make the platform work, it would all be for nothing, right? Instead, I want you to hear it directly from them–to feel what it's like to be in their shoes and to take comfort in their great skill and acumen!"

Phil, who was already taking detailed notes of the meeting, raised a knowledgeable smile. Yab took a bad situation and turned it into a tool. There was much appreciation and respect in Phil's eyes.

"So, guys," Yab said. "If you can, please explain how you joined the Spice Society and why you still choose to be part of it. I may ask a few important questions when the time comes. Pedro, please go first."

Pedro wasn't shy at all and eloquently took the lead, talking with great pleasure about his experience with and life in Spice Society. "I've worked with my father for several years now. Since I decided to join the fields–as the demand for hands and work has doubled thanks to the Spice Society–we have been working exclusively with Yab to grow plant proteins. I remember meeting Yab many years ago, when he was only first starting out, and we were one of the first families he approached. My father, like a typical, stubborn farmer, was very hesitant at first, but thankfully, we didn't pass on the opportunity."

"What can you say about Spice Society to Mr. Howard?" Yab asked.

"We learned so much from Yab and Spice Society," Pedro said. "We diversified our plants, instead of just growing chili peppers. We always obtain our seeds from Yab's team, and they have never failed us! The most important thing for us is the team of engineers Yab has assembled. Whenever we have a problem or a question, they're always there, kindly explaining everything about the diversification and the new processes we're using. We doubled our profits in the first few years, and I think we can do even better than that." We're thrilled to be part of the Spice Society, and having access to the best seeds and technical support really creates strong roots for our endeavors."

There was genuine enthusiasm in Pedro's voice, and true admiration for what Yab had offered them. Mr. Howard seemed impressed, but he wasn't yet convinced.

"What about the risk mitigation problem?" Yab asked.

"We live here, and we always have our ears nailed to the ground, listening to everything that's brewing. You guys hear the news only after things have already gotten out of hand. Here, we anticipate these things and adapt our business plans to make the company thrive despite whatever roadblock that might come up...sometimes literally as you can see." With this, Pedro gave a timid laugh. "Today, for example, my dad and I took the liberty of sending an additional 30 percent of our harvest to Yab's emergency stockpile. I just spoke to the driver, an experienced one, who took the emergency route through the fields we have been using for years, and he will soon arrive at Spice Society's processing plant. The people and government support what we do, and that means everything."

Mr. Howard nodded, now resting his hand against his jaw, thinking intensely.

"Thank you for letting me be part of this meeting and for hearing me out," Pedro said and leaned back with a satisfied smile.

Yab nodded with admiration for Pedro's presentation. His dad, Mr. Rodriguez, was very risk-averse, doubting the entire collaboration even after agreeing to join Spice Society.

It was men like Don Constantino and Mr. Rodriguez that made Spice Society what it was today. If not for them, Yab wouldn't be able to pursue his dream and raise the platform from the ground up.

After Pedro's powerful declaration, Howard's response to the presentation became something secondary to Yab; he was simply proud and grateful for the fruit of his work and this meeting basically turned into an opportunity for Yab to hear out what each part of the team had to say about Spice Society as a whole. He quickly snapped back to reality and saw Gustavo smiling widely on the screen; "Gustavo, you're up," Yab said, encouraging the boy that was now a fine young man, to take the lead.

Gustavo was a little hesitant at first, but as he started talking, his confidence grew. "I first met Yab in the caravan, when my brother and I decided to run away from our home as teenagers," Gustavo started. "We had nothing but a change of clothes. Yab took good care of us. He bought us shoes, and after we arrived in the US, we had the luck of being in the same city. He would drop by the orphanage, cook for us, and he was an inspiration for all of us back in the day. He even inspired me to go to college."

Gustavo stopped and took a deep breath. Remembering the old times brought tears to his eyes. "I managed to get into college and I graduated," Gustavo said with pride. "I had opportunities to work for many companies back in the US, but I decided to return home, to pursue the American Dream here, in the Mayan lands, where I belong. I trusted Yab, and I can see now more than ever that coming back was the right thing to do, as I have the opportunity to have an honest job that I really like.!"

"Like Mr. Rodriguez's family, Yab offered us a place in Spice Society's family, to put our land to good, profitable work. We had great success, and my other brothers no longer see the caravan as an option.

You see, there's no reason for us to run away anymore," Gustavo said. "I'm the plant manager here, and I'm also the official English translator thanks to my experience in the US. I'm honored to be a part of this united family, and I truly hope my kids can one day help make this platform grow even more! Let me also state here, as a witness to Yab's character, that my children are currently attending the bilingual school Yab set up for the community's kids. You see, this man doesn't just want to run a company; he wants to contribute and create a community that cares; and he's managed to achieve that so far; at least he's got me convinced of it. Spice Society is our family, and like a true family man, he does everything to protect it and see it thrive."

"What about the risk mitigation plans?" Yab asked.

"As Pedro said, he sent out the stockpile reserve because we all anticipated this turmoil. We're already two steps ahead and very **disciplined in our work.** The US warehouse should receive a large inventory cushion tomorrow. The 30 percent Pedro mentioned–that was just today. We've been ahead of this situation for quite a while now!"

Gustavo sat back again with his cozy new office on the back and wearing a buttoned white "Spice Society" shirt. Yab couldn't help but appreciate where Gustavo was now and feel grateful. The kid Yab had once met in the Caravan, barefoot and lost, was now one of the best plant managers he had ever seen.

The hardships in the US, along with the formal education and discipline he had received had shaped Gustavo into an invaluable candidate many companies around the world would die to have. Yab only hoped more kids would be able to follow the American Dream in the Mayan lands, without having to suffer as he, Gustavo, and his brother had.

"Victor," Yab said.

"Finally!" Victor said, rubbing his hands together. "Mr. Howard, I'll be honest. I discovered Yab, you know. Phil still owes me for that one, eh? I made these guys famous!"

Mr. Howard looked puzzled at Phil's loud laughter.

"Jokes aside, Yab actually made *me*," Mr. Victor said. "I wanted to hire a cook, and this man poured his heart and soul into my restaurant, working as if it was his own. He's given me only his best work, always, better every time. From the sauce to the recipes, this young man has been nothing but professional with a stellar performance!"

"Silly me, I had the idea of selling the sauce," Victor said. "But they would have thought of that sooner or later. I know a lot of restaurant owners, and the sauce is killing it in all those restaurants. Many friends of mine have turned their business upside down with **Spice Society's help and food expertise.** You'll be in the best hands possible with these guys, for real. They always let their fire and passion show through their hard work. Honestly, I don't know what they do down there–what contingency plans they have set up–but they're definitely one step ahead. I, for one, have never experienced any delays or hiccups, political instability or not!"

Yab and Victor exchanged a look that spoke volumes. They both had a deep and profound admiration for one another. It all started with Victor's restaurant, the catapult to all of Yab's success. Even at the beginning, when Victor was hesitant and stingy, he always treated Yab like the son he never had, and Yab couldn't thank him enough for that. If not for God's mysterious ways, which led Yab to meet Mr. Victor, Spice Society never would have been possible.

Yab shook off the emotional tears ready to burst, looking at Mr. Victor's proud smile–an expression that Yab had only seen on his parents' and his Abuelo's faces.

"Before this gets messy," Yab laughed, "why don't we give the floor to Carlos..." They all smiled. "Carlos, my good friend, you are up next," Yab said.

"Well..." Carlos chuckled, a little nervous.

It was the first time all of them spoke directly to one of Yab's investors. Victor and Pedro were more eloquent than Carlos, but he still managed to deliver a powerful message; he took a deep breath and started sharing his side of the story.

"I had the blessing to meet Yab in Culinary School," he said. "We always admired his resilience, kindness to others, and hard work despite his personal circumstances. I remember when Yab first visited as a guest listener. Since his first day there, he displayed the effort and nerve of a true warrior, earning the respect of the entire school. He was always grounded, and when you had trouble with something, he was the first one to try and help you, even before the teachers. He wasn't there just for the degree or the fancy title. He was truly a devoted man...obsessed even...with *knowledge*–not just his but everyone's–and that's what we admired about him!"

"Enough about me, Carlos," Yab said with a shy smile. "Tell us about your role in Spice Society!"

"Oh, yeah, right. Well, after our amazing though challenging experience in culinary school, Yab reached out to me a few years later, pitching me the concept of Yab's Chicken and Mayan Corner in New Jersey," Carlos said. "It was a wonderful idea and one I could replicate in many locations. I truly believed in the concept of traditional and plant-based Mayan recipes served under one roof where immigrants and locals could get to know each other and their cultures. Being a native of Mexico myself, my family and I are huge fans of Mayan recipes. *Pollo chuco* is a star seller–I'll tell you that. My father is more obsessed with eating that than with my mother's cooking."

Carlos took a quick breath and continued. "To conclude with what really interests you, Mr. Howard," Carlos said. "Yab's recipes are truly one of a kind, and our teachers at culinary school all agree. But it's not just that. Many tried to recreate the recipes with their raw materials, but the results simply aren't the same. Spice Society's ingredients are top-notch, and there's a huge difference in how Yab and these good men and women here do their work, overseeing the quality from the beginning until the end–from the farm to the table. Of course, I've never had an issue with the supply chain. From what I understand, Yab and Phil want to do more processing stateside, and from what I've seen so far, I can only anticipate more growth!"

Yab felt honored to hear Carlos speak with so much passion and such loving words for him. Yab remembered how shy and nervous he'd been the first time he stepped into culinary school. He had his janitor's uniform on, and he received many weird, even mocking looks from some of the students–but not Carlos. Carlos had always given him a hand when Yab was in need, and Yab had, ever since, always returned the favor.

It was one of the first days of class, and Yab had walked in late because of his janitorial work. The assignment had already been handed out, and Yab didn't have enough time to prepare. Some of the students couldn't help but show their discomfort. They probably meant no harm, but his presence made them uneasy. However, there were others, such as Carlos, that felt admiration for Yab, and in contrast to the other students, Yab's presence made him feel grateful for how easy things were for him. Carlos, big and brawny as he was, shot his classmates a livid look, silencing them for good, and he approached Yab with a wide smile. Carlos explained everything about the assignment and even helped Yab find the equipment he needed.

Yab ended up cooking the best dish amongst all the students there, even though he was half an hour late, thanks to Calros' eagerness to help. Their friendship started that day, with Yab and Carlos growing close, exchanging notes and tips, helping each other grow and become the best versions of themselves. Even to this day, Carlos was still one of Yab's best friends.

"Excuse me guys," Yab said quietly. "There's no way of not getting emotional, I'm sorry"

"Clarisa…" Yab cleared his throat, shaking the beautiful memories of the past away. "Just as we do in our restaurants with our desserts, we end on a powerful note!"

"Hello, everyone," Clarisa said, flashing her gorgeous smile. "I met Yab when he was a janitor at my school, not long before he met Carlos! I don't know if he ever told you that, but Yab used to sneak into the food lab on Saturdays to work with our top-notch equipment to perfect his sauce, and I'm so glad he did!

"Did you create this sauce by sneaking into a lab?" Howard asked, almost in disbelief.

Yab only nodded with a cunning smile.

"One time, I caught him by accident and he offered me a bottle for my silence," Clarisa said, laughing. "Of course, I wouldn't say anything, as he always kept everything clean and tidy, but how could I say no to free sauce? Whenever he worked on it, he would come and hand me another bottle, so you can say that I was his quality assurance department at the time!" Clarisa said with a sweet laugh. "I love chilis, so I always asked for the hottest bottle."

"Anyway, I recently moved to New Jersey, where I own a supermarket chain. You can't imagine my surprise when I saw Yab step into my supermarket and ask if he could sell the sauces and spices. Yab's sauce in *my* supermarket! Ever since he first shared his culture's wonderful flavors with me, it has always brought me great pleasure to share these awesome products with the mainstream consumers. Their reaction when they try them is priceless. So, the idea of helping Yab bring these flavors to a new country, for my American friends to try, was simply too good to turn down–how could I say no? I had no doubt, but quite frankly, I quickly learned that my expectations fell short regarding the sauce's impact on customer demand. We have to restock the shelves with Yab's sauce once, maybe twice a day! The customers are insatiable, but thanks to these impeccable gentlemen, we always have enough stock on hand! So, you can say that the collaboration is working well enough, and this experience has taught me to take more risks on innovative products! It's definitely been a win-win situation." A brief silence followed Clarisa's detailed explanation. "Go Yab!" Clarisa exclaimed and laughed to break the silence.

Yab looked at all the familiar faces, a **big family of smiles and success,** now working together in unison, bringing forth their best selves and pushing each other to become even better.

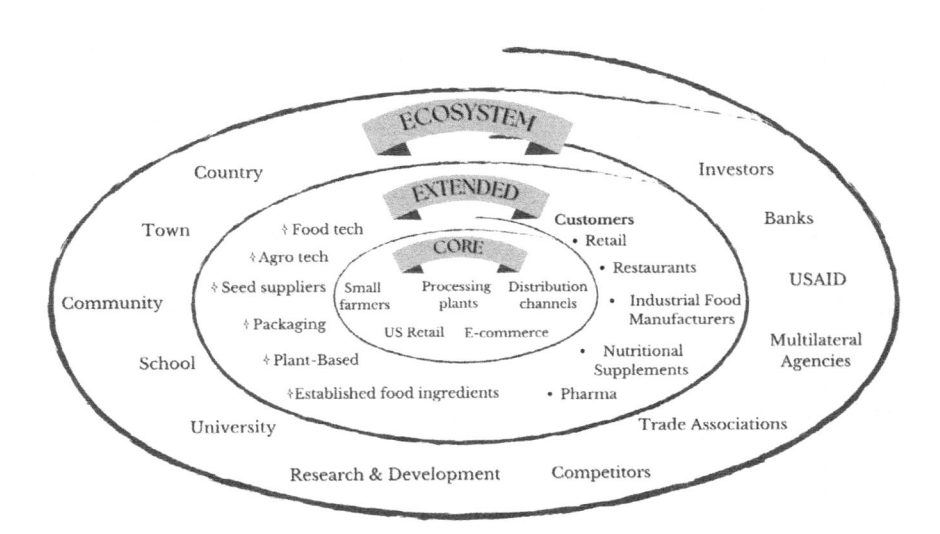

"Well, there you go, Mr. Howard," Yab said. "I'm proud that our beloved members of Spice Society were here for you to see how we conduct our business. Yes, there are risks, and there are always risks in the business world. If there's no risk, it wouldn't really be a business proposition, right? But I can promise you and all of the members here can guarantee that our current income combined with our unstoppable ambition to improve product quality, our clear purpose of serving people, and our legacy are worth the risk! Hope you can join us to help more families in Latin America, to **expand our family,** and achieve greatness…together."

"I'm in," Mr. Howard said well before Yab had finished his sentence. "I was a little hesitant at first, but no more! I saw initiative, imagination, creativity, and above all, hard work! You have a partner, Yab, and I say that with great honor."

The meeting ended with Mr. Howard inviting Phil and Yab for a nice dinner whenever they found themselves in the US, to highlight their ever-growing and continual collaboration. Everyone left, except for Yab and Phil, who stayed a little longer at the virtual meeting. Phil had never appeared more proud.

"Impressive maneuver there," Phil said. "Even I couldn't have done that better."

"Well, you taught me quite a lot," Yab said.

"I'm proud of you, you know. I don't know what the future will hold. Whether it's instability or climate change, anything can happen, but I do know that you're not alone. Oh, and one last thing, Yab," Phil said hesitantly. "I've discovered an important truth today, something that has made me feel more confident than ever of being by your side in this huge business endeavor."

Naturally curious, Yab gave Phil a half-smile. "Oh yeah, well I'm all ears."

Spice Society process circle (clockwise from top): SOWING, GROWTH, CROPS, HARVEST, PROCESSING, AGING, PREPARATION, BOTTLING, EXPORT, VALUE, SUPPLY CHAIN, RETAIL, ONLINE ORDERS.

Phil started, "I was taking notes of everything said and can summarize why Spice Society Platform is bound to be successful: 1) we use **world-class** seeds, which produce the strongest roots, giving a solid foundation to everything we do, 2) our **honor** comes from giving the best we have at work, and we do it with **discipline,** 3) we have **expert knowledge of our products:** spices, chili peppers, and plant proteins,

4) **our strategy is replicable** in many markets, and we're able to attract talent, and finally, 5) we're like a family and truly care about everyone's **wellbeing.**

Yab was absolutely surprised and humbled. At this point, he was hugging the ceiba tree's trunk as much as he could, as it was massive. He responded, "You just summarized my family's creed for work, and I'm here under the ceiba tree. Surely the platform will work. I had my doubts but this is a clear sign it will be successful. It has definitely been the result of a constant attitude of the heart; and the result has been overwhelmingly powerful: a business platform bigger than any of us that has proven its potential to provide abundance for many and that still has a long way to go."

Phil, still inspired, said, "Yep. Out of all the things I imagined that I'd do, I would've never predicted I'd end up building a bridge–such a beautiful one…bigger than any other bridge in the world…one that not only connects two masses of land but cultures–and *families.*"

• • •

After the meeting concluded, Yab sat down with his back against the tree, gazing at the alluring scene unfolding before him. His smile was restless, and his heart was still pounding. Another obstacle had been conquered, another challenge overcome. The investor seemed pleased with the presentation, securing his stay with Spice Society. They had many challenges ahead of them, as they always did and always would, but Yab had claimed yet another victory, honoring his promise to all the good people working with him once again. Their families would grow and prosper, as long as Yab never gave up trying, always facing any new challenge with the same amount of enthusiasm and resilience he always did.

Yab had held the spinner throughout the entire meeting and only until now realized as much. Looking at its beautiful texture and vibrant colors, Yab thanked the spinner for its valuable help.

Slowly raising his gaze, Yab noticed his Abuelo's house, and then he remembered his obligation toward him. Yab hadn't picked up the spinner that day because he foresaw trouble. No. He had a duty toward his Abuelo and his cousin, but first, he had a quick stop to make.

Yab got back into his car and drove toward the outskirts of Copán where Manuel's father had his souvenir workshop. Yab entered the store of beautiful ornaments and souvenirs, a tapestry of the Mayan history, and greeted Manuel's father.

"Hola, señor," Yab said and bowed.

"Yab!" Manuel's father exclaimed, wiping the dust from his hands. "How can I help?"

"How's the shop going?"

"I can't complain," Manuel's father said. "The business is good, and people love the souvenirs!"

"I heard you have the best souvenirs in town," Yab said.

"Manuel told you that?" Manuel's father and Yab shared a laugh. "What brings you here?"

"I want you to replicate this relic," Yab said, showing the spinner to Manuel's father.

"No problem, Yab! How many pieces do you need?"

"Fifty thousand!" Yab said.

The man's jaw dropped, "You're serious…"

"Yes! Fifty thousand, I'm sure you can handle it!"

"Of course I can. the number just caught me by surprise."

Manuel's father studied the spinner, drew it on a piece of paper, and took all the necessary steps to replicate it perfectly even without the real one in his hands.

"What are you going to do with so many, anyway?" Manuel's father asked.

"I'm going to write a book and give one out to my first fifty thousand readers," Yab said with pride.

"A book? A book about what?" Manuel's father asked.

"Many things, many things," Yab said. "Just wait until you read it! Thank you for accepting my order. We'll talk again soon."

It was finally the time for the hardest part of the journey–the return to Abuelo's home.

Yab hesitantly got inside the car and slowly drove toward his Abuelo's house. Up the hill, through the rainy, mist-engulfed scenery, Yab saw his Abuelo's adobe emerging through the thick foliage.

It had been a while since the last time he had visited. Nostalgia and a surge of feelings overcame Yab's mind. This is where everything began: the first revered lessons, his merchant's graduation, the temple, the power of manifesting, and finally, his trip to the US. It had all started here.

I've been through so much, Yab thought as he stepped out of the car and reached for the fence surrounding Abuelo's cottage. He had grown and learned so much. He was an idealist, as Dominic always said, but a proactive one, always with a win-win-win mentality in mind, giving him power and purpose.

"Yab!" his Abuelo called from the garden at the house's side. "Are you dreaming again?"

Yab chuckled, "No, Abuelo…just remembering the old days."

Yab approached his Abuelo, who was inspecting his chili peppers.

"What were you thinking about?" Abuelo asked.

"Mostly how much I owe you," Yab said.

"Owe me? What are you talking about?" his Abuelo asked, almost insulted.

"For teaching so much–to formally set goals through the spinner and constantly perform the discipline of manifesting my Mantra," Yab said. "I know I have a long way to go, but you gave me the tools I needed to move forward!"

"Nonsense," Abuelo said. "You owe me nothing, my boy. I taught you all that as it was my duty to do, and one day you'll teach those things to your grandchildren, and only then you will understand my true motivation; pure love for my favorite grandson!"

"Thank you, Abuelo," Yab said. "I feel more mature now than ever before."

"You truly are, and that's why, I think it's time for you to pass on this legacy, the spinner I gave you, to your cousin!"

Yab frowned, taking the spinner from his pocket, staring at it, probably for the last time.

"Do I have to, Abuelo?" Yab asked.

"Yes, you have to!" Abuelo said. "You have grown and matured, you have learned, and the path before you is now vivid and clear. There will be difficulties but nothing you can't overcome and conquer on your own. Your cousin is still young, and now we need to pass to him what was once passed to you; the spinner will help him now as it helped you all this time. He needs this tool to guide him through the dark, to show him the way as it did with you! Your cousin is seeking to discover his self-efficacy like you did. Hand it over now. I can't imagine a better moment!"

Yab hugged his Abuelo, clenching him tightly as the boy he once was, hugging his Abuelo when scared or uncertain. Tears overwhelmed Yab's eyes. It felt like another chapter between them was coming to its end, and Yab wasn't ready for that. The spinner was his guidance, and it felt like a bridge between him and his Abuelo. Yab wasn't ready to part ways with it. It was a safety net, a useful tool always accompanying him. Yab was afraid of what the future would hold without it.

"Don't worry, Yab," Abuelo said, immediately sensing his distress with a soft, warm chuckle. "Nothing's over. This is only the beginning, you know."

Abuelo looked him in the eye and wiped a single tear from Yab's cheek with his thumb and pointed at his heart, tapping it softly with his index finger. "What are you, Yab?" he asked.

Yab smiled through his sorrow. "I am God's Temple," Yab said with a sniff.

"And who's inside you, Yab, at all times, every waking moment of your day and night?" Abuelo asked.

"The Holy Spirit," Yab said, his smile growing warmer at the realization.

"Go on then, my boy, and show others how to produce their intended results using your experience with the Mayan spinner. You have a lot of work to do, and you're just getting started. I can see inside you glory, success, and happiness, and remember that my predictions rarely are incorrect.

"Now go and grow your platform!"

These words made Yab remember a very important thought.

"Abuelo! We both almost forgot about my homework." He took out a rare looking type of paper fiber, rolled up like a scroll. Abuelo smiled as he saw that Yab had honored his request; he had drafted the ten most important takeaways of his trip, but what really blew Abuelo away was that Yab did it on mayan paper–known as HUUN in mayan language– made of plant fiber pulp. "Where could he get it from?" Were Abuelo's thoughts.

"Oh, and… since I know you're probably wondering, I got the HUUN from Manuel's father at his shop. Great guy; he asked for you by the way. You should pay him a visit."

Aware that he was living out one of those moments that the mind and the heart immortalize, as his grandson walked away, frozen in awe, Abuelo opened the scroll from end to end, and read through it.

> 1. Embrace your origins.
>
> 2. Be skeptical. Always double-check what you perceive to be true.
>
> 3. Having strong goals will create a clear vision.
>
> 4. Trust your creative mind.
>
> 5. Be kind to others, as there is always someone with a greater need.
>
> 6. Become an expert at something that you are passionate about.
>
> 7. Constantly update what you know (navigate life with a humble learning attitude).
>
> 8. Partner up and share experiences.
>
> 9. Create opportunities for your community.
>
> 10. Your mindset should be set to do business anywhere.

Proud of himself, Yab took a deep breath and looked out upon the vast expanse of fields unfolding beyond where the eye could see.

My father was right, Yab thought. *Everything I needed was already here.*

But this wasn't a call to sit back and relax. His true calling was rather to take this beauty and share it with the whole world.

The End

ABOUT THE AUTHOR

Rodolfo, better known as Rudi, is a Central American-born entrepreneur from a German - Honduran marriage rooted in strong Catholic values, with business operations in the United States and Spain. Over his twenty-seven years of experience Rudi has been involved in Commercial Banking, Satellite Communications, Retail Food, Functional food ingredients, Agrotech and family office investments. Since 2014 Rudi has lived abroad in Miami, FL putting into practice his entrepreneurial skills to generate opportunities for his homeland and his people.

Always concerned about social inequality and the consequences it has in Central America, he has been a volunteer to his community as the Founding President of United Way Honduras (a non-profit that's focused on early childhood) and the ex-president of "Asociación Nuevo Amanecer", a bilingual vocational school that serves an underserved population in Central America. He has also Chaired YPO in Honduras and Miami.

"Holcan Code" is his invitation for anyone interested to join the fight against stagnation in Central America!